SHADOW
OF THE
GALLOWS

CALIBER
BOOKS

Also from DOYLE TRENT

CHAPTER 1

From his cell in the Fortune city jail he could hear the hammering.

Every nail driven, every board sawed, meant he was closer to the end of his life.

Guilty, the jury had said.

Hang by the neck, the judge had said. And may God have mercy on your soul.

Mercy. He shook his head sadly. There was no mercy in Fortune. Too many robberies. Too many killings. Too many innocent folks living in fear.

Someone had to pay. Someone had to hang.

Tom Shannon sat on the steel bunk and put his face in his hands. He wished he could shut out the hammering and sawing.

It was only a week ago that he had been sentenced by a solemn-faced judge from Fairplay. At first he'd had hope. Someone, somehow, would discover the identity of the real killer.

"I'm no murderer," he had protested.

No one listened. No one cared. Except Mary. The Widow Cress.

She couldn't hold back the tears the first time she visited him in jail, and when he was sentenced to die she had burst into tears inside the courtroom.

Courtroom? Hell, it was the back room of the vacated bank building. There was no courtroom in Fortune. The jury—six stalwart men—listened to the evidence and were asked to vote. Those who thought him guilty were asked to step to the north side of the room.

All six stepped to the north side. The hammering went on.

"Won't be long now."

Tom looked up at Deputy George Atwell, a paunchy man in his early fifties. Handlebar moustache. Rounded shoulders. A look of fatigue always on his face. He stood in front of the cell. "I'm going to get you some supper. It's your last meal, so you can have anything you want."

All Tom could do was shake his head.

"You ain't et all day."

Still Tom said nothing.

"Well, don't know as I'd want anything to eat either. It'd be kinda hard to swallow."

When his prisoner remained silent, Atwell went on, "It's a shame about you, boy. I kinda liked you. I wouldn't a guessed you to be a backshooter."

Tom stared blankly at the deputy and said nothing. What could he say that hadn't been said.

"Well"—Atwell turned to leave—"I'm just doin' my duty."

"Mr. Atwell." Tom spoke now, and the deputy looked back. "Will you do something for me?"

"Try to, boy. Anything within reason."

Shannon stood and came over to the cell door and looked between the bars. "Will you try to keep Mary from..." He didn't know how to say it.

"Shore, son." Now the deputy was talking like a father. "I know what you mean. I'll get Mrs. Atwell and some of her friends to stay with her."

"Thanks."

Friends? No one had any real friends in Fortune. No one trusted anyone.

Outside, the hammering ended. He looked up at the narrow window high over his head, and the angle of the shadows told him it was getting late in the day. The gallows had to be finished by daybreak next morning, and they couldn't work in the dark.

Then he heard the sound that made him flinch. It was the *spang* of a heavy spring pulling a trapdoor down. He heard someone yell, "It

6

works."

The gallows was finished.

Every man in Fortune would be up early next morning to watch the execution. Even a few women. It would be the first execution in Fortune. Fortune, so named because men had found gold and silver in the hills to the north. Men were getting rich in the mines. But so were the thieves. The mercantile, the saloon, the Silver Lode Gate, the hotel, the blacksmith, all were built at the foot of the mountains, where traveling was easier. Fortune was the only settlement between Fairplay, sixty miles to the west, and Tarryall, fifty miles to the east. Traveling the Ute Trail wagon road between Fairplay and Tarryall had become dangerous lately because of the thieves and killers. They'd kill a man for what they could find in his pockets.

Tom took hold of the windowsill with his fingertips and pulled himself up to where he could see out. The gallows stood close to his window, between the jail and a laundry where the less fortunate women worked. It was stout, with pine timbers for a frame, thirteen steps leading to the plank platform, and a headframe above it all. Like the headframes on the mines.

Thirteen steps. They would be his last steps.

The first day after he was sentenced, Tom had paced his cell like a caged raccoon. He swore, then asked the Creator for forgiveness for using his name in vain. He sat, smoked, and paced.

By the second day he was calmer, beginning to resign himself to his fate. He had even shaved with a borrowed straight razor, and bathed out of a bucket of cool water. He almost didn't recognize himself in the small shaving mirror.

Tom Shannon had always been given to thinness, and his face had always been lean, with a wide mouth and square chin. His pale blue eyes went with the sandy hair he had inherited from his Irish ancestors. Now his face had the resigned, lifeless look of an animal that had been caged too long.

Nobody was going to admit murder, not even to save an innocent man. No witness was going to come forth and exonerate Tom Shannon. Hell, there was no witness.

But on the third day he was nervous again. He paced, smoked until his head ached and his throat was raw from smoking, sat, paced. If he could get out, he might, somehow, find out who the killer was. How? Hell, he didn't know. He was no detective.

On the next day, he went over it all in his mind for the fiftieth time, step by step. Someone had shot Scott Wheeler. Who? The sheepherder? No, the deputy admitted the sheepherder had had a reason, but he'd been liquored up and passed out in the Salty Dog saloon all night. He couldn't have done it. Who else? Zack Parmell, foreman on the Wheelers' Running W Ranch? He had come to town with young Wheeler that night, but witnesses said he was playing poker when Scott Wheeler was shot.

Scott Wheeler hadn't been a bad guy when he was sober, but when he drank he'd never been able to stay away from the card games, getting mean when he lost. In fact, he'd always been mean when he drank. Had he lost that night? According to witnesses, not much, if anything. Or maybe he'd won, and somebody'd wanted his money back and had been willing to kill to get it back.

But at the trial, Atwell testified that he had checked into that and had learned that young Wheeler had just about broken even in the faro game and had started for home about ten o'clock. Nope, the deputy said, everything pointed to Tom Shannon.

Too many men had seen him and Wheeler face each other, ready to fight. They'd seen Wheeler threaten him with a gun and then had heard him call Tom a coward for not carrying a gun. They'd seen Tom leave the saloon, and now they figured he'd gone home, got his old Civil War Enfield, and waited outside in the dark for Wheeler to leave.

They all testified to that. No one testified on his behalf. Except Mary, and all she could say was Thomas Shannon was not the kind of man to shoot someone from ambush.

Tom Shannon had no alibi. His story that he'd gone back to his one-room cabin was too easy. Too pat. And if he hadn't done it, how had an expended percussion cap from his long-barreled rifle come to lie at the scene of the crime? No one had seen another rifle of that kind in the South Park country of Colorado Territory.

It was easy to see where the killer had waited in a dark alley, smoking and stomping out his cigarettes on the ground. Two shots had been heard five to ten seconds apart. It was plenty of time to fire, reload a percussion rifle, and fire again. The percussion cap was there. And someone remembered hearing a horse leave on a gallop, heading east in the direction of Tom's homestead.

That's all it took.

Now Tom Shannon, who had survived the War Between the States, the bloody fighting at Shiloh along the Tennessee River, and more skirmishes than he wanted to remember, who had fired hundreds of rounds from his Enfield rifle and had hit dozens of men, was about to die for a shooting he hadn't committed.

Soon after daylight, his life would be over.

He wanted to see Mary one more time, and yet he didn't. He didn't want to see the anguish in her face, hear the pain in her voice. This was harder on her than on him. Had he been given a choice, he wouldn't have seen her again.

But he had no choice.

Her voice came through the door between the deputy's office and the one-cell jail, and it was the voice of determination. "I'm going in there, Mr. Atwell, and that's final."

The door burst open and she was there, the deputy right behind her. "Tom." She was standing before the cell door. "I had to come, Tom. I..."

Her voice started to break, and he could see her square her shoulders, blink back the tears and force herself to talk in a normal tone. "I wanted to bring you something special to eat, but Mr. Atwell wouldn't allow me to bring you anything."

She glanced over her shoulder at the deputy.

"Don't blame him, Mary. He offered to get me anything I wanted, and he can't have you handing me anything between the bars." A grim smile touched Shannon's lips. "He's afraid you might slip me a gun."

She reached between the bars to touch his face, and the deputy interrupted. "Don't do that, Mrs. Cress. You're not allowed to touch." She paused, then touched him anyway, her fingers fluttering over his cheek.

Deputy Atwell didn't try to stop her, but stood behind her with his thumbs inside his gunbelt, watching intently.

"Mary." Tom considered his words carefully. "There's something I want to say." Another grim smile turned up the corners of his mouth. "There's a lot of things I want to say, but mainly I want to tell you to forget about me. Go on with your life. Pretend I didn't happen."

"I can't do that, Tom." She stood there now like a broken rag doll, her neat brown hair parted on one side, her wide gray eyes full of hurt. Tall for a woman, slender. "You know I can't do that."

He pleaded. "You have to, Mary. Don't let this ruin your life. Go back to Iowa. Don't stay here. You've got to, Mary."

She answered in a small voice. "All right, Tom, if that's what you want."

"You're not just saying that, are you, to make me feel better?"

"No."

He studied her face, the nice angular face with the firm chin and mouth. "Then, it's settled? You'll go back to your hometown in Iowa?"

"Yes."

"I...I'm sorry, Mary. I'm sorry I caused you ill this grief. I wouldn't hurt you for the world."

"I know you wouldn't, and I know you didn't shoot anyone in the back."

"I didn't. Believe me, I didn't."

"Of course I believe you. I never doubted you, not for a second."

"It's good to know that."

"Tom." Her voice was back strong and her shoulders were squared again. "I'm not going to let them brand you a backshooter. I'm not going to let them do that. I—"

He could see the anger returning, the determination, and he had to stop it. "Mary. Mary, you promised. Don't let this make you bitter. Forget about me and go on with your life. You're a young woman and you've got a lot of living to do. Don't let this ruin you. You promised."

Her shoulders slumped again. "Yes, I promised."

She reached through the bars and touched his cheek again, then she turned and walked away through the door. Deputy Atwell followed her.

CHAPTER 2

Sit. Smoke. His eyes were tired from the lack of sleep, and his head felt as it were full of sawdust. Smoking too much wasn't good for him, he thought, then snorted. What difference does it make? What the hell is the difference?

Darkness came, and with it Deputy Atwell, carrying the lantern he always left four feet away from the cell door. The light and the steel bars in the door made thin, vertical shadows on the opposite wall.

Just sit there on that wooden bunk and wait for daylight and death. What else could he do? Escape? Bust out? He'd thought about it, tried to find a way.

The deputy's office and jail were built of huge timbers, squared and notched and fitted exactly. The steel bars were bolted through a timber that was at least eighteen inches thick. The floor was made of more thick timbers. No way of digging out or cutting through the walls. The window was too narrow for a baby, much less a six-footer like Tom Shannon, and that steel bar in it made it impossible for anything bigger than a pack rat to squeeze through. The ceiling? More heavy timbers. It was an escape-proof jail.

Not only that, Deputy Atwell was a careful man. He never entered the cell without drawing his six-gun first and ordering his prisoner to stand against the far wall. The old Negro swamper who came for the toilet bucket every day was never let in the cell until Shannon was against the wall, and even then Atwell kept a careful eye on him, his gun leveled, the hammer back.

There was just no way.

He sat on his bunk and smoked, coughed, and smoked. Why wait? A man could cheat the gallows and the spectators by hanging himself in his cell. He picked up one end of a worn and tattered wool blanket, one of two blankets on the bunk, and, just out of curiosity, tried to tear it. It tore.

Yeah, he said to himself, a man could tear up this blanket and make a rope out of it and hang himself. Wouldn't that disappoint all those bloodthirsty sonsabitches who wanted to see someone hang? He smiled a grim smile when he thought about it. It would be easy. Tie one end to that bar in the window, the other around his neck, and jump off the bunk.

Working silently, he tore one strip off the blanket, then another. Needed two more. He tore them off, keeping an eye on the door that led to the deputy's office. He tied the ends of the strips together. Now he had a rope. Was it strong enough? He put his booted left foot on one end, bent his knees, and passed the rest over his back close to his hips. He tried to straighten his knees. Couldn't. It was strong enough.

Now he could do it. The deputy was keeping an all-night vigil, but he wouldn't come back to the jail until daylight. That is, if nothing happened to arouse his suspicion. It wasn't long until daylight.

But did he want to do it? He sat on his heels on the floor and felt defeated.

No. He would climb those thirteen steps like a man.

Unless...

His eyes fell upon the remains of the torn blanket and the other whole one, and an idea began germinating in his brain. He turned it over and let it grow. It might work.

Moving fast, he rolled up the two blankets, stopped, listened. Footsteps? Moving fast again, he unrolled the blankets, spread them over the bunk, hid his makeshift rope under them and lay on them. The door opened and Deputy Atwell came through.

"Sleeping, Thomas?"

"Huh? Uh, not much."

"Soon be daylight."

"Yeah."

Atwell left, closing the door behind him.

Now was the time. Shannon rolled up the blankets again, tied one end of his rope around them about two feet from the end of the roll, and bent the end down. Not much of a dummy, but it might work.

Now he held the other end of his rope in his teeth, got his fingers on the windowsill, pulled himself up, got hold of the window bar with one hand, and slipped the rope around it. He dropped down, pulled the roll of blankets up to just under the window, and tied the rope to the wooden leg of the bunk.

Listening and watching the door, he stepped back, into the corner near the cell door. Yeah, it could be mistaken in the near darkness for a man hanging there, head to one side.

Now all he could do was wait.

That narrow window was fascinating to a man waiting for daylight. The lantern outside his cell door flickered and went out. The deputy had forgotten to fill the tank with coal oil. Dark now. Shannon watched the window, waiting for a sign that day was coming. It was a kind of terrible fascination, watching the light slowly change.

He was back in the wet woods along Owl Creek, waiting for dawn. Most of the night, Bragg's Corps had crawled through the woods to an attack position. The Yankee encampment was well-guarded, and success depended on surprise. Two hundred men shivered in the cold, damp, dark woods, rain driving into their faces. Soon after daylight the order would come to advance. There would be heavy enemy fire and the air would be full of exploding Minié balls. Lieutenant Thomas Shannon of the First Kentucky Brigade was one of the leaders. Men would die. He could die.

Tom Shannon waited. Slowly the night outside the cell window changed colors. Was he imagining it? He blinked and looked again. No, the night was changing. Soon, whatever was to happen would happen.

He tried to relax, to stay loose. When the time came he would have to move fast, and he needed all his reflexes. He swung his arms, trying to stay loose.

He could see light outside now. He heard men's voices under

his window. The crowd was gathering, eager to watch a man hang.

Footsteps in the deputy's office. The door opened. Shannon shrunk back in his corner as tightly as he could, hoping he wouldn't be seen from outside the cell. The deputy was coming, but then he stopped and went back through the door. What went wrong? Did something tip him off?

No, he was coming again, carrying another lantern. Shannon waited, breathing shallow breaths.

He heard Atwell gasp, heard him set his lantern on the floor, heard a key in the lock, heard the cell door open. Now. Move now.

The deputy was hurrying to what he thought was a man hanging by the neck, and when he discovered his mistake it was too late. Tom was behind him, an arm around his throat and his left hand grabbing for the six-gun on his hip.

Atwell let out a squawk, but the gun barrel pushed against the small of his back and Tom Shannon hissed through clenched teeth, "Shut up. Keep quiet. One sound and I'll blow your spine in two."

A strangling sound came from Atwell's throat and he was quiet.

"All right now. Down on the floor. Face down. Hands behind your back."

Shannon pulled his makeshift rope down from the window bar and used it to tie the deputy's hands and feet. He tore off another piece of the blanket, rolled the deputy over and stuffed it in his mouth, tied it there with a piece of his rope.

Got to move fast, he told himself. Men will be coming to help the deputy bring the condemned prisoner out. Got to get out of here fast. He ran through the connecting door into the deputy's office, grabbed Atwell's felt hat and a rifle, looked out the window in the semidarkness at the men gathered around the gallows, and hurried to the back of the room and a back door.

Almost afraid to breathe for fear of being heard, Shannon pulled back the wooden latch on the door, cracked it open, and peered out. No one in sight. He gripped the rifle in his right hand as he slipped out, staying close to the building in the shadows. The best place to go, he decided, was into the foothills. He knew that part of the country and the high hills well after running cattle there for two years. If he could make it to the hills he could find a place to hide.

He kept his back against the building and made his way to the corner. The crowd was on the other side near the gallows. Looking ahead, Shannon picked out the dark side of a pole barn as his next stopping place, then ran, keeping low. There, he stripped and listened. All he heard was the snorting of a horse in the barn. A horse. He needed a horse.

But he was on the wrong end of the barn. The door was on the other end, in sight of the men and the gallows. He couldn't risk it, and he ran low to the shadow of another building, then another and another, until he was out of town.

Now he ran as fast as he could without looking back. Get to the hills, off the sagebrush flats, he thought. Stay low, stay away from the road, and run Tom ran, carrying the rifle in one hand and the deputy's six-gun in the other. His boots, made for riding, not walking, clomped over the ground, through the sage and around the soapweeds. His breathing was becoming painful, and his lungs were pumping dangerously fast. He had to stop for a moment.

But when he paused, bending low, and looked back over the top of the sage, he knew he couldn't stop. Men were standing behind the deputy's building, looking around. They would know he was headed for the hills, and they would get horses and come after him. He couldn't outrun horses.

Run. Get up there where a man could climb hand over hand, where the horses couldn't go. Or better yet, get into the buckbrush. He ran, his lungs hurting, his heart pounding. When he came to a ravine, he jumped into it, knowing it would lead to the brush and from there to the hills. He ran along the sandy bottom until it shallowed out, and then he was in the scrub oak, so thick that a man on a horse had a hard time riding through it. A cow could get in those forty or so acres of scrubs and hide where an army couldn't find her. He knew about that because he had chased cattle through it and had torn his shirt and scratched his face every time. Now he would use that to his advantage.

At times he had to get on his hands and knees, keeping his hold on the rifle, and push his way through. After he'd gone five hundred yards into the scrub he felt safe. Now he could stop and get his wind. He lay on his back and rested, willing his breathing to get back to normal.

It was broad daylight now, though the sun still hadn't shown itself over the eastern hills. Another grim smile touched his lips when he saw, in his mind's eye, the townsmen running and riding off in all directions trying to find him. The whole town of Fortune, all three hundred residents, would be excited. The condemned man had escaped.

And Mary. She would be happy that he had escaped, but she would be worried too. If they caught him, they would hang him immediately. If they didn't catch him, he could get lost in the mountains and die of starvation, or freeze to death, or... A lot of things could happen.

Now he could hear them. They were far enough away that he couldn't understand what they were saying, but he could hear the excitement in their voices. A horse nickered. They were mounted. They suspected he was in there.

At first Tom thought he'd better get out of the brush and get to the higher hills. But on second thought, he realized that's what they expected him to do, and that in a short time they'd have the scrubs surrounded so tightly a man couldn't get past them.

He was trapped.

CHAPTER 3

He crawled on his hands and knees again, looking for a better place to hide, careful not to touch the trunks of the scrubs and cause a ripple at the top. He heard a horse crashing through behind him, and he lay face down.

The rider was swearing. "This goddamned thicket. A rabbit couldn't get in here." He yelled, "Hey, Zack, see anything?"

It was Zack Parmell, foreman of the Running W, who answered, "No, goddammit. Go slow. You can ride right over him without seeing him."

He stayed where he was until the sound of horses went on past, then crawled another fifty feet and came to a narrow draw. In it, on his back, he would be impossible to see unless someone stumbled over him. He lay on his back and listened.

Voices. "I'd bet a double eagle he's in here somewhere."

"He's in here, all right. We've got more men coming. We'll find him."

"Gotta get on foot. Can't ride a horse in here."

"I'm walkin' and leadin' my horse."

"I ain't walking."

He knew the foreman wouldn't get off his horse. A cowman didn't believe in walking as long as he had a horse to ride. But others would. If there were enough of them, they might stumble over him. And soon there would be a lot of men pushing through the scrubs. Every miner, cowboy, and timber cutter would join in the sport of chasing the most exciting game of all—a man.

All Tom Shannon could do now was wait for dark. After dark he might slip out of the scrubs and get past them. Once in the high hills, he could climb the ridges where a horse couldn't, and he had a good chance of staying away from them. He lay on his back—he wanted to see them before they saw him—and waited.

How had it all started, anyway? Had he done something wrong? Yeah. What he'd done wrong was to stop Scott Wheeler from beating up an old man. It was in the Salty Dog saloon...

He had stopped outside the saloon with V.C. Wheeler, who owned the Running W Ranch, and who was the father of Scott Wheeler. Shannon had a half-shorthorn bull that Wheeler, a middle-aged, portly man with thick shaggy eyebrows, wanted to buy. He wasn't interested in selling, and told the rancher that.

"Hell, V.C., you're getting the benefit of him anyway. I'm riding most of the time, trying to keep my stock away from yours, but every time I look up I see a Running W cow."

"How many cows can that bull service in a year?" V.C. asked.

"I don't know. Maybe fifteen or twenty."

"How many cows have you got now?"

"Forty-two head. And twenty-four calves and another bull."

"Your other bull hasn't got the breeding of that big white son-of-a-buck."

"No, but he can make babies, and that's what the cow business is all about."

"Tell you what, let's go in here and have a drink and talk. I might make you an offer you can't turn down."

Tom had to accept a drink of whiskey just to be neighborly. It was late, and he'd just left Mary and was on his way home, back to his one-room log house and his log corrals and log stock shelter. He had mixed feelings about V.C. Wheeler. The man was the first stockman to settle in the South Park country and he boasted that it all belonged to him. But so far he had made no threats.

They went into the Salty Dog and stepped up to the bar. Wheeler ordered whiskey and added, "Some of that good stuff. None of that rotgut." The barman, a tall thin galoot with a prominent Adam's apple, served the best whiskey he had. The saloon was one long room with a pine-board bar on one side and tables on the other. A faro table stood at the far end, and the dealer, a dandy with slicked-back black hair, a thin moustache, a flowery vest, and a pearl-handled pistol carried low on his right hip, was a permanent fixture. There was space for dancing, but there were no women to dance with.

"Now," V.C. said, "let's be reasonable. You've got forty-two cows. At last count, that is. And two bulls. Now, if you got a good calf crop last spring, then I'll bet some of your cows got serviced by one of my bulls."

Tom grinned. "Unless a bull elk got hard up."

V.C. was serious. "Now, what is beef on the hoof selling for?"

"Last I heard, it was four bits on the pound."

"Now then, what will your bull weigh?"

"A good fifteen hundred, and he's all beef."

"Suppose I offer you a hundred bucks for him. What would you say?"

"I'd say that'd be a fair offer if I wanted to get out of the cow-calf business—but I don't, and I need that brute."

"Hell, son, you could lose him. Larkspur kills a lot of cattle up there, and there's lots of other ways cattle can die. Believe me, I know. When a damned cow gets it in her head she's lived long enough, nothing can keep her alive. And it's like you said, no matter who owns that bull, he's going to service all the cows he can and he don't look at brands. Your S Bar cows could still have his calves."

"No." Shannon grinned again. "You'd keep him way to hell over yonder somewhere."

"Have another."

"Let me buy."

They talked for an hour or so, and finally the older cowman gave up and left. The Salty Dog had filled up, and among the latecomers were Scott Wheeler, the young cocky offspring of V.C. Wheeler, and Zack Parmell. Parmell spoke to V.C. Wheeler, his boss, but young Wheeler acted as though he didn't even see his father. Both men were armed, and young Wheeler carried his six-gun low on his hip. Tom had heard—the whole county had heard—that young Wheeler was always practicing with the gun and was handy with it.

"Hey, Shannon" Wheeler yelled down the length of the pine-board bar.

Tom was about to leave. "Yeah?"

"I hear you've got some competition for the Widow Cress. I hear some big son-of-a-bitch timberjack is courtin' her."

Shannon knew he was being hoorawed, and he didn't much like it, but he didn't want to fight over it either. He shrugged and said nothing.

"I hear that son-of-a-bitch's hung like a government stud."

Now it was getting dangerous. He couldn't ignore a remark like that—He had to ignore it. He turned to go.

"Hey, Shep." It was young Wheeler picking on someone else, now that Tom had ignored him.

Tom had seen the old man with the long gray beard drinking alone at a table on the far side of the room. No one knew his name, but everyone knew he herded about a hundred sheep in the hills northeast of Fortune. He stayed up there with his sheep, two dogs, and two horses, and lived out of a wagon with a tarp cover. The cattlemen didn't like it, but it was a free range and the sheepherder had as much right up there as anyone.

The old man knew he was being addressed and he looked up with bloodshot eyes.

"Is it true you sheepherders diddle your sheep?"

The old man downed what was left in his whiskey glass and smiled. It wasn't a friendly smile. Tom stopped near the door and listened and watched, wondering what was going to happen next. He guessed then that the old man wasn't as old as his long beard, rounded shoulders, and baggy bib overalls made him look.

"Hey, Shep. I'm talking to you. Is it true what they say? Do you diddle those ewes?"

The smile inside the beard widened, and the sheepherder's voice came out loud and clear. "Hell yes, son, where do you think our little cowboys come from?"

Guffaws broke out of the crowd of men in the Salty Dog, then cutoff immediately when the men saw the mean look on Wheeler's face. In a few long, quick strides, Wheeler was at the sheepherder's table. He grabbed the old man by the front of his overalls and hauled him to his feet.

21

"What'd you say?" he yelled. "What the hell did you say?" His right fist smashed into the sheepherder's nose, and blood began pouring out.

"Say it again. Go on, say something like that again. I'll teach you to respect your betters."

It was a useless try, but the old man put the palm of his hand against Wheeler's face and shoved with surprising strength. Wheeler staggered back and almost fell, then recovered his balance and charged, fists swinging. The old man went down. The toe of a riding boot pounded him in the side. That was when Shannon got into it.

Looking back, he knew he should have stayed out. It was every man for himself in Fortune. No one knew who his enemies were or who his friends were. Someone was killed every week or so, either in a fight or in an accident, or by the gang of thieves. Carrying money and letting it be known was asking for death, and fighting with an armed man was asking for death. But he did it anyway.

He grabbed young Wheeler by the arm, spun him around, and jerked him aside. "Don't." That was all he said.

In a flash, the six-gun was in Wheeler's hand and the hammer was cocked. Tom could see death coming, and he backed up a step, not breathing. Wheeler raised the gun to eye level and aimed it at the bridge of Shannon's nose.

Someone said quietly, "He ain't armed."

"Why ain't you packing iron?" Wheeler hissed. "You afraid of guns?" When Shannon didn't answer, he went on, "A man carries iron. Only a coward goes around without a gun."

Still no word from Tom.

"Why don't you go get a gun and come back, Shannon. I'll be here waitin' for you." he sneered. "Are you too scared?"

For what seemed like an hour the two men stared at each other, neither backing down. The whole room was quiet. Everyone was waiting for the boom of the six-gun and the death of the cowboy from the cedar hills.

Finally, knowing he could be shot in the back, Shannon turned and walked out. His steps were slow and his knees were weak. He half-expected to feel the slug tearing into his back. The door seemed to be a mile away. Finally, he was there and through it and out into the sweet night air. He couldn't hold back a sigh of relief as he went to his bay horse tied to a hitchrail and mounted. The hair on the back of his neck seemed alive as he rode slowly out of town.

That's how easy it was to get shot to death in Fortune. Thinking back, Tom guessed that young Wheeler didn't want the reputation of a man who shot an unarmed enemy in the back. But he knew then, not guessed, that the time would come when he and Scott Wheeler would fight, and he knew that only one would survive.

They didn't come for him until early morning. He had shot a buck the day before, gutted it and brought it home on the back of his saddle. Fresh venison had tasted mighty good when he ate his supper after getting back from Fortune. He missed his dog. Old Ranger was so old he couldn't see much, and he'd finally lain down outside the door and died. If Ranger had been alive and well, they couldn't have sneaked in on him.

The first sound he heard was the double click of a gun being cocked. It took a second for the sound to work through to his brain and identify itself. Then he sat up with a snort, only to be hit on the head and knocked down again.

"Don't move," a harsh voice bellowed. "Move and you're a dead man."

At first he moved only his eyes and saw a half-dozen men around his bed. They were nothing but dark shadows in the moonlight that came through the window over his bed, but he knew they were men.

A match was struck and the lamp on the homemade table beside his bed was lit. He recognized Deputy George Atwell, three townsmen, and Zack Parmell.

"What...what's going on here?" he asked.

"I'm arresting you for the murder of Scott Wheeler," Atwell said.

"What?" He sat up, pushing the bed tarp and blanket down.

"You heard me."

"Scott Wheeler? Is Scott Wheeler dead?"

"You know damn well he is," Atwell said. "We believe you

shot him."

"I didn't. I didn't shoot anybody."

"Get your clothes on. We've got a place for bushwhackers like you."

By daylight he was locked up in the Fortune jail, and two days later he was tried before the district judge who had just finished presiding over a trial at Fairplay. He was to hang a week later.

The ground was cold, and the sun was late coming up. Tom Shannon couldn't stop shivering there in the shallow draw. Winter wasn't far ahead, and the nighttime temperature would soon drop below freezing in the high hills. Whatever he did, he had to get out of the mountains before winter, had to get his cattle out.

Yeah, and how the hell was he going to do that? A hunted man couldn't do much of anything. His cattle would drift down themselves, and with him not there to gather them they would mix with the Running W cattle. Eventually, with no one to claim them, they would belong to the Running W.

Well, he had other things to worry about now. Like how to get away from a bunch of armed men and survive. Like where to go if he did get away. Like what to do about Mary.

Mary had suffered enough in her twenty-nine years to last a hundred. First, her husband Billy Cress was murdered by a gang of thieves that was just beginning to terrorize the South Park country of Colorado Territory. Then, fourteen months later, while she was earning a living waiting tables in the Silver Lode Cafe, she had gotten acquainted with Tom Shannon and seen a future with him. Tom, the war veteran who had come to South Park driving a small herd of cattle and six horses, including two percherons with harness and a packhorse loaded with camp supplies, who had homesteaded a hundred and sixty acres at the foot of the mountains east of Fortune and had built himself a cabin there.

Living with Tom Shannon would be a hard life, but she was more than willing. His herd would grow and he'd buy more cows, and one day he'd have his own S Bar Ranch.

Now Tom Shannon was about to die too.

What to do about Mary.

CHAPTER 4

When the sun did come up, it warmed things some and Shannon was grateful for that. He could hear men pushing their way through the scrub oak, but none came close. He tried to decide what to do if a man came onto him. Would Tom shoot? He'd have to if he wanted to live. But could he do it? As the day slowly passed, he thought about that question again and again. The men looking for him were mostly honest, hard-working miners and cowboys, and they were doing what they thought was their duty. If justice was to come to Fortune, the thieves and killers would have to be caught and hung. Tom hoped he wouldn't have to shoot, but he was determined that he wasn't going to hang.

His stomach reminded him that he hadn't eaten in over twenty-four hours, and he wished he'd taken Deputy Atwell's offer of a fine last meal. It was midafternoon now and the searchers hadn't given up. He heard more voices. "He's got to be in here somewhere."

"Shore he is, but an elephant could hide in here."

"Well, keep your trigger finger ready. We know he's got two guns."

It was uncomfortable, lying on his back on the hard ground, but he didn't dare move. Then it was turning cold and that meant the sun was low in the sky. Come on, darkness, he said to himself. Was it finally getting dark? Stay still. Won't be long now. His stomach grumbled from the lack of food and he couldn't stop it. Quiet, dammit, he muttered under his breath. Yeah, it was getting dark. Dark and cold. He shivered, and felt so stiff he wondered if he could move when the time came. Slowly, darkness arrived.

He waited until it had been dark for at least an hour, then got stiffly up. He stood in the scrubs and swung his arms and stamped his feet to get the blood circulating and to stop shivering. When he left his shallow draw he headed east, ducking low and sometimes crawling on his hands and knees, still hanging onto the rifle. The searchers were probably there, forming a ring around the forty odd acres of scrub oak, but he believed he could slip past them in the dark. There weren't enough men in all of Park County to form a tight ring. Had to be quiet, though. Not a sound.

His knees were sore from walking on them over the hard rocky ground, but he knew he was close to the edge now and didn't dare stand up. Moving slowly, he crept on. Now he heard men talking in low voices. He couldn't see them, could only hear them. He crawled closer until he saw the glow from a cigarette. That gave him even more hope.

They weren't soldiers. A soldier would have been court-martialed for talking and smoking on guard duty. These men weren't trained for guard duty. Now that he'd spotted them, Shannon knew he'd have to crawl farther to get around them, and that took more time and made his knees painfully sore.

He was out of the brush and crawling into a deep ravine that slanted uphill. Still crawling, he got to the top of the ravine and guessed he was about forty feet above the brush. He stopped, sat on the rocky ground, and looked back. It was a black night, and he couldn't see them, but he knew they were there. Were they smart enough to station a few men uphill from the scrubs in case he came that way? Tom didn't know, but he knew he was going to have to keep on moving quietly. Any sound would arouse suspicion.

He crawled another hundred yards, bumped into a tree, crawled around it, and bumped into a granite boulder. The ground in front of him slanted sharply upward. He stood and walked, holding the rifle and his left hand out in front of his face, trying to feel the tree limbs and boulders before he bumped into them. He believed he knew the hill he was climbing, and if he was correct, it went to the top of a long pine-studded ridge. From there the land slanted down into a narrow valley, and across that was another ridge.

Climbing was hard work, but he knew a horse couldn't follow him up that hill. He considered leaving the rifle behind to make climbing easier, but decided to keep it. A good gun could save a man's life in more ways than one. So he climbed, using his left hand to grab tree roots, rocks, bunch grass, anything he could get hold of to help pull himself up. Hard work, but better than lying in that brush back there. At least he was moving and no longer cold.

His scrambling loosened a few rocks and they rolled downhill, making a racket that couldn't be missed by the men below. Sure enough, a man's voice cried out, "Hey, there's something up there. He's up there."

Tom hugged the ground as a dozen rifle shots split the quiet night. One bullet sponged off a rock near his left foot and another thudded into a tree off to his right.

Dammit, he thought, can't scramble up this hill in the dark without making a noise. Got to get up this hill. He waited, flattened out, heard a voice yell, "Did you get 'im?"

"Hell, I don't know. Won't know till mornin'."

"Maybe it wasn't him. Coulda been a buckskin or somethin'."

Shannon climbed. A few more shots came his way. Then he was at the top of the ridge. He sat there on the ground and reached for his tobacco. No, that wouldn't do. Might, just might, be someone up there. Got to keep moving. But Lord, could he ever use a smoke.

Going downhill was easier, and noisier, but he had to put some distance between him and Fortune and he couldn't do it crawling. A tree limb knocked his hat off and he lost three minutes searching the dark ground for it. When he found it he walked and slid faster. At the bottom, he stopped again. He knew that each hill he climbed would be higher than the previous one, until he reached the top of the pass; then, each hill would be lower until he was down on the Ute Trail wagon road. He wouldn't dare travel the wagon road, and he still had no idea where he would go.

His feet were wet from splashing across a narrow creek when he started up the next high hill. A quarter moon came up over a ridge to the east and put out enough light that he could see the black shape of the trees.

Not worried about making a noise now, he climbed hand over feet, tripping over roots and rocks, and in another hour made it to the top of that hill. Now he had to stop. His legs were giving out and his empty stomach made him feel weak. Scooting on the seat of his pants, he found a flat spot just under the hill and rested. There couldn't be another human for miles, and he took out his tobacco sack and papers and rolled a cigarette. Not much tobacco left, and not many matches. How many? He groped his pockets. Only one. One match. Can't use it now. Might need it later. He put the cigarette in his shirt pocket.

The night wind sighed in the tops of the pine and spruce, and now that he was sitting still, Tom shivered in the chill of the night. He stood and waved his arms to keep warm, then started walking and sliding downhill again. It occurred to him that a man could break a leg or an ankle scrambling around in the rocks in the dark, but there was nothing he could do about it. He kept moving.

After getting down from that hill and climbing another, he had to stop again. By then he was too tired to go much farther, and he found a level spot under a pile of huge boulders where he could lie down. Within minutes the chilly air got through his thin shirt and he couldn't help shivering. He lay on his side, pulled his knees up and put his hands between his knees for warmth, and finally the fatigue outfought the cold and he slept.

The sun didn't show itself that morning. The sky was overcast and the clouds were so low he couldn't see the top of the next ridge. Cold. Cold enough to snow. Shannon stood and looked around. He waved his arms and stamped his feet and tried to stop his teeth from chattering.

Then he picked up his guns and made his way downhill. At the bottom, he pushed through dense willows to a trickle of a stream, lay on his stomach and drank, then squatted and splashed cold water on his face. He believed he was far enough from his pursuers that he was in no danger from them. Now he had to find a way to survive.

And that, he knew, wasn't going to be easy.

CHAPTER 5

How long could a man live without eating? A long time. But Tom Shannon knew that each day he went without nourishment made him weaker, and that eventually he would become so weak he could do nothing but lie down and wait for death. He sat on a rock on the side of a grassy hill and considered his predicament. He believed he knew where he was even though the low clouds shortened visibility to no more than fifty feet. No one could find him in that weather. But he still had to eat.

He was in a valley between two high ridges, and the valley was filled with mountain vegetation. There were the remains of summer's wild flowers, and there was the bushy cinquefoil. None of it edible. The willows were still in leaf, though the leaves were yellow and falling. No nourishment there. That stream that ran through the willows wasn't deep enough to hold fish.

Tom remembered the chokeberry bushes that grew along a creek not far from his cabin and he remembered seeing a black bear stuffing itself on the bushes. But he had been warned that only a bear could eat it. Even a horse could get sick on the chokeberry bushes.

Trying to subsist on wild vegetation was foolish. Too much of it was toxic, and unless a man knew exactly what he was eating, he'd be better off going hungry. Going hungry made a man weak, but dysentery made him even weaker.

There was wild game. Deer and elk, rabbits and squirrels. Wild turkeys. Hell, a man could eat a chipmunk if he was starving. He levered the cartridges out of the rifle and counted them. Seven. They were .44-40s. The gun was a Winchester model 1866, brand new, a good gun. Better all around than his old Enfield. Why, he asked himself, hadn't he traded off the old war weapon long ago for one of the modern guns that fire metallic cartridges? Maybe it was because he had lived with it for so long he hated to part with it. Yeah, that was the answer, but that was foolish. A percussion cap from the Enfield was easy to identify. It was the most damning piece of evidence against him. Well, too late to do anything about that now.

He reloaded the Winchester, and then remembered he didn't have a knife. Deputy Atwell had emptied his pockets and left him with only his tobacco and matches before locking him up in the jail. He should have thought of that and looked around the deputy's office for a knife when he broke out. But then, the oversight could be excused. After all, he'd been in a hell of a hurry. Now he had two guns with which to kill game, but no knife. What could he do, kill something and butcher it with his teeth?

Tom Shannon ran it all through his mind and realized he had three options:

He could go back to his cabin. Lord, could he use that mackinaw hanging on a nail in his cabin, and some jerky and bacon and canned beans and fruit. But they probably expected him to go back and they would be waiting for him.

Or he could wait for dark and sneak into town. Mary shared a four-room frame house with another, older widow, and if he could somehow attract her attention she would give him something to eat and a blanket. But he didn't trust the other woman, and asking Mary for help would be putting her in danger. There were laws against helping fugitives from justice. Deputy Atwell was a vindictive son of a bitch, and he'd give her a very hard time.

That left only one other. He could make his way to the wagon road running east and west and try to stop a wagon and bum something to eat. That would be risky too. If he stopped a wagon going west, the traveler would go on to Fortune and tell about the half-starved man on the road, and Atwell would gather a posse and come after him. If he stopped a wagon going east, the traveler would have just come from Fortune and would recognize him.

All right. Shannon stood and stretched. He had to do something, and he was going back to his cabin. He had food and blankets in his cabin, and there was his stash. He had buried his money behind the cabin because the bank was robbed so often that money wasn't safe there. And keeping his money hidden turned out to be a wise decision because the bank had closed its doors and gone out of business two weeks ago. Too many robberies.

He would have to approach his cabin with a lot of care. If it was being watched, he'd have to change his plan. The fog would help. Maybe, under cover of the fog, he could at least get to his stash. He'd rather buy food from a traveler than bum it.

Tom had ridden the country he was in and he knew the game and cattle trails, and that made traveling a hell of a lot easier than climbing mountains. He walked quietly and kept his eyes glued to the trail ahead. There was little chance of meeting any human there, but he was no gambler. His stomach was growling like an angry animal, and the weakness at the pit of his stomach was spreading to his knees and legs.

When he got to the lower elevation, the fog thinned but still limited visibility to a hundred yards. Tom Shannon knew exactly where he was going. He guessed it was about noon when he got to the timbered hill on the north side of his homestead. He stopped at the top of the hill.

On a clear day he could have seen his cabin and corrals from there, but not today. The fog blanked out everything from the bottom of the hill on. Tom sat still and listened. His cabin was a quarter mile away, but sound carried far in the high, thin air. He listened and heard nothing. Sitting still made him shiver again, and he would have given anything for the mackinaw he had hanging on the wall in his cabin. And the bacon and the canned beans and tomatoes. And matches. A stiff, chilly wind came up behind him, and he knew he was going to have to have that mackinaw.

Well, he didn't come here just to sit on top of a hill in the wind and the cold, misty fog. Moving as quietly as he could, he made his way down, still carrying the rifle. He had to come down the hill with his feet turned sideways to keep from sliding. In spite of that, he slid at times, and each time he loosened a few rocks that rolled with a clatter down the hill ahead of him. That always brought him to a halt and caused him to strain his ears and listen. No voices. No sound at all.

The closer he got to the bottom, the slower he moved and the more often he stopped. Finally, he got down to level ground and crouched in a shallow, rocky ravine. Then, ears and eyes straining, he walked, keeping low, toward his cabin, ready to bolt and run.

If his cabin was watched and he was spotted he had a chance of escaping again in the fog. No, on second thought, if he was spotted he probably wouldn't even know it. There would be no warning, no "Halt, who goes there," or anything like that. He would be shot on sight.

The hair on the back of his neck was alive again and his heart was in his throat as he crept on, eyes and ears straining. Why couldn't he see the cabin? The fog was thick, but he could see the twisted junipers on the east side of the cabin.

He crept on, stooping low, stopping every few steps to listen and look. He smelled smoke. A shift in the breeze brought the acrid, sickening smell of charred wood.

"Oh, no," he muttered as he quickened his steps. Then he saw the cabin. It was leveled. Not a stick standing. Only the stone fireplace and chimney. Just a charred, black mess. His three-sided stock shelter was burned too, and his corrals were flattened on one side. Everything was destroyed. He was sick. He sat on the ground and fought down the nausea. Everything he had worked for since staking out the homestead two years ago was gone. For a long while he sat there, feeling the way he had felt when President Jefferson Davis had given up and he'd known the Confederate States of America, the nation thousands of men had died for, was no more.

Then, moving in a daze, he poked through the ruins of his cabin. The smell of charred wood burned his nose. His eyes watered. The east-iron stove had survived and so had the steel bed frame. That was all. The canned vegetables were swollen out of shape and he knew the heat had changed the bacteria and made them unfit for consumption. Out in the stock shelter, he found his set of harness a black, twisted mess. A crowbar had survived, but a shovel handle had been burned off. Someone had made certain nothing of value was left.

When had this happened? Just yesterday? No doubt. While the whole town was looking for him, had him trapped in the scrub oak, someone had come here and set fire to everything that would burn. The smoke had to have been seen from Fortune, and he wondered if anyone had come to see what was burning. No way of knowing.

Poking with a stick among the ashes of his cabin, he found a blackened tin plate, some eating utensils, a butcher knife. The wooden handle of the knife had been burned, but the knife was usable. He carried it in his left hand, the stolen rifle in his right, as he prowled through the ruins. Then, satisfied that nothing more could be salvaged, he went out to the largest of the half-dozen junipers east of the ruins and used the knife to dig under the largest root and uncover the coffee can.

Inside the can was his money. Two hundred and twenty-three dollars in paper U.S. treasury bills. Money he had worked and sacrificed for. Only he and Mary knew about it. He had told her during one of her visits to the jail. She should have it, he said.

She had been surprised at the amount, but he'd reminded her that he had worked for six months in the bottom of a gold mine, mucking the fractured rocks, and had spent two summers working for wages in the timber, using his team of percherons to drag logs out of the woods onto a road where they could be hauled in wagons to the sawmill. He had spent only a small part of his wages, and was saving to buy more cows.

Now, if he could get to some faraway town, the money would keep him eating until he found a job and a new career. Mary would be more than willing to go with him if he could slip into Fortune and see her. But no, that wouldn't do. He would always be a wanted man and would always be looking over his shoulder. That was no life for Mary. She could do better without him.

Tom Shannon put the money in the pocket of his denim pants. He put the butcher knife inside his belt at the back and put the six-gun inside the belt on his left side. He had to tighten his belt a hole to keep everything in place, and he thought grimly that if he didn't eat soon he'd have to tighten the belt another hole to keep his pants up. Walking right along and carrying the rifle, he stayed at the bottom of the hill and headed east. He stayed away from the two wagon ruts that led to his cabin and away from the Ute Trail road that went over the pass to the cities on the eastern slopes of the Rockies.

His plan now was to get as far east of Fortune as he could walk—at least twenty miles—then make his way to the Ute Trail road and stop a westbound wagon. With his money he could buy something to eat and a blanket.

Just before he walked out of sight of what used to be his home, he stopped and looked back. He spoke two words:

"Good-bye, Mary."

CHAPTER 6

Lord, he was hungry. He walked around the bottom of the piny hill and into a valley, climbed a rocky ridge and slid down the eastern side of it. Now he believed he was far enough away from civilization that he could fire a shot without it being heard. The mountains were full of game, weren't they? No, not always. Sure, he had seldom had to buy meat, except for bacon, but there had been times when he had carried his rifle with him looking for meat and failed to find any. In fact, there were weeks when he didn't see a thing to shoot. Where was everything now? Only a couple of weeks ago he had seen squirrels everywhere, carrying pine cones, readying for winter. Squirrels carrying pine cones were a sure sign of fall. Now there wasn't even a chipmunk.

He was so hungry he believed he could eat anything. Even a raven. There were always the ravens. Except now. Maybe when the sky cleared he'd spot something. Hell, he could walk within fifty feet of game in this fog and not see it. Looking up, he cursed. Dammit, clear up. A man has to eat. Lord, he was hungry.

Just before dark he had to make another decision. Another night without food or shelter could leave him so weak he wouldn't be able to go on, yet he also knew he had to get farther from town before he went down to the Ute Trail road.

All right, he told himself, here's the plan: he had to keep warm. If he didn't he could die of pneumonia. And he had to eat. He had only one match. So what he'd do was build a fire, stay up all night feeding the fire, and in the morning go looking for game and try to kill something and dress it out and cook it over the same fire. That would give him strength to travel on.

He reached for the one match he carried in the sweatband of his hat, the only place he could be sure of its keeping dry in the damp, misty weather. Under an outcrop of granite he found some dry, dead grass, and he pulled it up by the handful. He pulled grass until he had a pile about a foot high. Then he broke dead branches off the lodgepole pines, thankful that the lower branches of those trees were always dead. He shaped his pile of grass carefully under the outcrop, then took another look at his match.

The match was dry, but he remembered someone telling him once that a match rubbed through human hair was more likely to burn. Natural oil in the hair made it burn better, he'd been told. He rubbed the match twice through his hair. "Now," he muttered, "it comes down to this."

Kneeling before his pile of grass, he struck the match on a rock. It flared. Immediately he cupped it in his hands. It burned. Carefully, he held it under the grass. The grass caught fire. Afraid to breathe, he watched as the fire grew, flickered, almost went out, flared again. "Come on," he said under his breath.

The grass burned and the fire grew until he thought it hot enough to burn damp wood. He hoped it was. He started with two small sticks. They smoked. The fire almost went out. He blew gently on it. It flared again and the wood smoked again. "*Come on*," he muttered.

It took time and patience, but eventually he got more wood smoking, then finally burning. He added to his fire carefully, believing too much damp wood would smother it. The fire was good. He could feel heat from it. He added more until he had a big fire, one that warmed his whole body. Using only a pinch of his tobacco, he took out the cigarette and lit it with an ember from the fire. It tasted good and he drew the smoke deep into his lungs. Now he wanted daylight and something to shoot.

But daylight was a long time coming, and he had to stay awake and keep the fire going. With feet feeling like lead weights and legs rubbery with weakness, he walked around, broke branches off the lodgepoles, and stacked them near the fire where they would dry. Between forays for fuel he rested and smoked the last of his tobacco. In the morning he would find something to shoot, and he would eat and then he would walk to the road and try to stop a westbound wagon.

Soon after that, when the wagon reached Fortune and the driver told about him, men would be looking for him on the road, and he would have to stay in the hills. Walking wasn't his favorite method of transportation, but if he could buy food and a blanket he could walk to the next settlement. There he hoped he wouldn't be known, and could catch a ride to some city on the eastern slopes of the Rockies. Or buy a horse. It would take several days to walk to the next settlement, but he believed he could do it. It was his only chance.

Just before daylight, he dozed off, sitting with his back against a boulder, but he woke up with a snort in time to keep his fire from dying. He checked the load in the rifle and waited. At daylight he went hunting.

It was another cloudy day, but the fog had disappeared during the night and the clouds were moving, an indication that it might clear up.

After an hour of walking in a quarter-mile circle around his fire, he was discouraged. He had seen nothing alive at all. He couldn't go too far from his fire and let it burn out. He walked a little farther and still saw nothing. Not even a bird. He was about to give up and start the long walk to the road on a starving stomach when he heard a raven.

The big black bird flew overhead and made its croaking, cawing noise before it lit on a branch near the top of a ponderosa. Tom had never heard of anyone eating a raven, but anything was better than nothing. He sighted along the barrel of the rifle. His hands were shaking, and he had to lower the gun, take a deep breath, and try again. Hunger had left him so weak he couldn't hold the gun steady. He lowered it, breathed, and tried again. Finally, he squeezed the trigger.

The boom of the rifle echoed back and forth among the hills for what seemed like long minutes. The black bird fell off the tree and didn't move. Excited now, Tom hurried to it and carried it back to his fire. The .44-40 slug had almost butchered the bird for him, but he cut it open and cleaned out the remaining entrails. Pulling feathers off was too slow, and he skinned the bird, cut off a side, and tossed it in the fire. The smell of burning meat was awful.

Swallowing an uneasy lump in his throat, Tom waited until the meat was dark brown, then dragged it out of the fire with a stick. He picked it up, blew ashes off it, and took a bite.

Lord. He almost threw up. He waited until the sickness in his stomach subsided, and took another bite. Boot leather would have tasted better. The thing to do, he decided, was to chew and swallow as fast as he could. That way, maybe, he wouldn't taste it. He tried. It still tasted terrible. Bite, chew, swallow. He finished that half of the bird and skinned the other half and threw it in the fire. He ate that too, feeling even sicker. His stomach threatened to throw it all right back up.

Weak with sickness, Tom Shannon lay on his side with his knees drawn up and groaned. He clasped his hands across his stomach and thought again he was going to die. He wished he could throw it up and get rid of the taste. He got to his knees and tried, and couldn't even do that.

He was on his knees trying to vomit when he heard the clatter of horses' hooves on the rocks. He looked up and saw two riders coming. They had guns in their hands.

CHAPTER 7

No one spoke.

The two sat their horses, six-guns pointed at Shannon. Tom got slowly to his feet, feeling dizzy, facing them. He saw no badges. They had several days' growth of whiskers, and there was no way of telling from their clothing what kind of work they did. One wore a dirty gray shirt with no collar, striped wool pants, and low-heeled jackboots. The other had a duck jacket, bib overalls, and lace-up boots. The man in the gray shirt wore a wide-brimmed hat with the brim turned down all around, and his partner had on a pillbox cap with a bill. Both had pistol holsters strapped around their waists, and rifles in scabbards under their right legs. Their horses were both bays.

Shannon stared wide-eyed at them. Their faces showed nothing. Finally, one of them spoke. "You et a crow?" He was looking at the remains of the raven.

Nodding his head weakly, Shannon said, "Yeah."

The man in the wide-brimmed hat got off his horse and stepped closer, studying Tom's face. "You're him, ain't you?"

Tom said nothing. The man looked at his partner. "He's the one busted jail over to Fortune." Looking back at Tom, he said, "Ain't you?"

There was no use denying it, but still Tom hesitated. The man walked behind him. Tom didn't move. His rifle was picked up, examined, and his pistol was taken from his belt.

The man in the cap, still on his horse, spoke for the first time.

"Your name Shannon?"

"No, uh..."

"The hell it ain't." A grin creased his face. "You done busted out and took off a-runnin'. Just afore they was a-fixin' to hang you."

"They said he shot somebody in the back," said the other.

"No," Tom protested. "I didn't shoot anyone."

"You was tried accordin' to law and you was gonna hang."

"I didn't do it."

"Way I heared it," said the man on the horse, "they're blamin" him for shootin' that snot-nosed kid, that Wheeler kid, the one's been tryin' to show how tough he is."

"Oh, him."

"Plugged 'im in the back one night. So they said."

In spite of his illness, Shannon was damned tired of being called a backshooter, and his anger rose in his throat. "No, by God, I didn't do it."

A chuckle came from the horseman. "That's what you been a-sayin', but nary a soul believe you."

No use arguing. He glanced around, trying to find a way to escape. The man behind him had his guns, and the horseman in front of him had gun in his hand. "Who are you? Are you cattlemen?"

That brought a guffaw from the man on the horse. "Yeah, that's what we air. Way I heared it you're a cowman too."

"Yeah." Tom tried to place the accent. Kentucky?

"There's a difference twixt us. You raise 'em and we steal 'em."

"What?"

Another guffaw. "You didn't think we was the law, did you."

"No, I, uh..."

"You so hongry you was eatin a crow?"

"Yeah, uh, there was nothing else."

"Ain't got no horse nor nothin', huh?"

"No."

"Way I heared it, you took off afoot. You're him, all right."

Tom noticed without interest that his fire was dying. It didn't matter now. All he could do was stand there, feeling sick to his stomach.

The two were silent a moment, and the man behind Shannon stepped in front of him, gun barrel pointed at his chest. He had Tom's stolen six-gun stuck in his belt.

"Mebbe what we oughta do," said the man on the horse, "is take 'im to town and turn 'im over to the laws." He haw-hawed. "Wouldn't that be a job? Us turnin' somebody over to the laws. Make 'em think we was law-abidin' citizens."

"Naw. I don't think he'd make it on foot, and my horse won't carry double and neither will that long-headed brute you're on. Best thing to do is put 'im out of his misery."

The one on the horse didn't comment on that. Instead, he said to Tom. "You was an officer, wasn't you?"

"What?"

"In the war. I can tell by the way you talk. Way I heared it they found a cap from a squirrel gun where that crazy kid was shot. They said you was the only one that carried that kind of gun around here. I usta have a gun like that."

"You did? You were in the war?"

"Yep. I fit with the Second Kentucky boys. What outfit was you in?"

"The First Kentucky Brigade."

"God damn. Way I heared it, you got the shit shot out of you."

"Yeah."

"Me too." The horseman half-turned in his saddle and pointed to his left hip. "Took a ball right here. Time I could git around agin, old Jeff Davis gave up."

"We're both lucky we're alive," Tom said, trying to keep the conversation away from the fact that he was at their mercy.

"Yeah, but I took a lot of shit from the officers." He paused to see if Tom had anything to say to that. Tom didn't. "But there was some good officers too. They got shot the same as the rest of us."

Shannon said nothing to that either.

"Well, shit, Sam'l," said the man on foot, "we got to get on down there. We can't be late. You know what he'll do if we don't show up when we're s'posed to."

"Yeah, that's a fact. We got to go. Nice talkin' to a feller Reb, but we cain't take you with us and we cain't let you tell about seein' us. So long, Reb." He raised his gun so Tom could look up the bore.

Tom glanced around desperately, looking for somewhere to run and hide behind. There were the boulders that had shielded his fire, but they were at least four steps away. Too far. Still, he couldn't just stand there and be shot.

"Wait a minute," said the other man. "Let's see if he's got anything in his pockets." He stepped close, shoved the barrel of his gun against Tom's stomach, and ran the fingers of his other hand in and out of Tom's shirt pockets. His breath smelled like something dead. "Nothin' there." He put his left hand in the front pocket of Tom's denim pants. "Oh-oh. What's this?"

He had Shannon's money in his hand. "Hey now, look at this, Sam'l. He's got a roll that'd choke a mule." He held the money up to show to his partner.

Tom saw a chance. Moving fast and with desperation, he grabbed at the pistol. He got his thumb between the cocked hammer and the cartridge, felt the point of the hammer dig into the flesh of his thumb, ignored the pain. He jerked the man forward with his right hand on the gun, grabbed him by the shoulder with his left hand, spun him around, and got his left forearm around the man's throat. No use trying to twist the gun out of the outlaw's belt.

A gun cracked. The man's knees buckled and he collapsed against Tom. Shannon squatted, got under him, got an arm around his waist, and held him up. With his other hand he tried to cock the hammer bank and take aim with the six-gun, expecting another shot from the horseman.

But the one shot had spooked the horse and it jumped sideways, then danced nervously, making itself hard to handle. The other horse was running downhill, bridle reins flying. Another shot cracked, and Tom felt a sharp, hot pain sear his left side. He let the wounded man fall in a heap at his feet and squeezed the trigger of his own gun. The gun bucked and boomed, but the horse had jumped sideways again and the bullet missed its mark.

Both men had drawn guns, but the horseman was fighting with his mount while Tom stood still, holding his gun out straight, aimed at the mounted man. He could feel a stinging in his left side.

"Drop your gun."

The outlaw knew Tom was in a better position to shoot, and he let his pistol fall from his hand. His teeth skinned back from yellow-brown teeth. "That dumb son of a bitch got his own self shot."

"Get down," Tom said.

"Cain't do that, Cap'n."

"Get down or I'll shoot you down."

"So long, Cap'n." He wheeled his horse around, touched spurs to it, and went downhill at a full gallop, following the riderless horse. Tom had the outlaw's back in his gunsights and his finger on the trigger, but he didn't shoot. He watched as the horseman caught the riderless horse by the reins and led it away.

The man at Tom's feet groaned and flopped over on his back. Shannon spun around and aimed his gun downward, ready to shoot if the man reached for a gun. But the man was dying. A red spot was spreading in the middle of his shirt, and his breath was coming in ragged, painful gasps. Tom ripped the shirt open, saw the entry wound just under the right breastbone, and knew it was a fatal wound.

He unbuttoned his own shirt and saw a red gash in his left side just above the belt. If the bullet had gone one inch farther to his left it would have missed. As it was, it had torn a small chunk of flesh off his side then smacked into the boulders at his back. The wound stung like a hornet's bite, but Tom knew it was nowhere near a vital organ. It would have to be attended to sooner or later, but there was nothing he could do about it now.

While he was inspecting his wound, the other man's breathing stopped.

What next? Tom asked himself as he stood there, still feeling sick. Leaning against the boulders, he tried to think. He snorted with sarcasm. Plenty of weapons. Three pistols now and the rifle. But nothing to eat. Nothing had changed, except that he had narrowly escaped death again, and a man was dead.

Tom Shannon knelt, picked up his roll of money, and went through the dead man's pockets. He found a sack of tobacco, a book of cigarette papers, and matches. In a hip pocket he found another roll of paper money. He counted it. One hundred and forty-two dollars. Too much money for a working man to be carrying. He stood and put all that in his own pockets. So he was stealing from a dead man. The dead man was a thief. The money had probably been stolen from someone else. And the dead man had tried to steal from him.

No use trying to bury the body. No shovel. Not enough strength to dig a hole in the rocky ground anyway. Move on.

Picking up the rifle, Tom decided to leave the two outlaws' six-guns on the ground. He didn't need them and didn't want to carry them. He walked.

CHAPTER 8

The dark clouds were moving now and for a few seconds the sun came out. It felt good on Shannon's face while it lasted. It gave him hope that the weather would clear. He headed east and south, planning to reach the Ute Trail road about the middle of the afternoon. By then he ought to be far enough away from Fortune that he wouldn't have to hide from the deputy and the townsmen.

He walked on, legs feeling weaker. The pain in his left side had settled into a dull ache. His stomach was still threatening to heave up everything in it. When he came to the bottom of a high steep ridge, he had to stop and sit for a moment. He rolled a cigarette from the dead man's makings and smoked. The smoke made him dizzy. Stubbing out the cigarette in the dirt, he stood and started climbing the hill.

It took a good two hours, climbing, pulling himself up with one hand, grunting, straining. He had to stop a half-dozen times and rest, and each time he didn't see how he could keep going. He had to keep going. At the top, he walked along the ridge, looking down into a wide, green-brown valley. His legs felt like wooden sticks and he had to order his feet to keep moving. "Lord," he said to himself, "when I get to the road I'll be such a sorry-looking sight I'll scare everyone who comes along."

It was noon—he could tell by the sunlight that shone through the clouds—when he stopped to rest again. His eyes took in the valley below. It was greenish-brown with autumn grass, and there were clumps of aspen trees that were mostly bare of leaves. A line of willows cut through the middle of the valley, and Tom guessed that a creek was hidden in the willows. It was a high valley. Tom could tell that from the sagebrush-like cinquefoil that grew on the far side of the willows. In the summer those bushes were green with tiny yellow flowers, but now they were mostly brown.

And to the south were a hundred or so small white boulders.

Suddenly Tom's eyes narrowed. The boulders were moving. He wiped his eyes with a shirt-sleeve and looked again. Yes, they were moving. What the hell? Then he recognized them. Sheep. He walked to a higher point where he could see better, and watched. Sure enough, a sorrel dog ran around one end of the herd of sheep, and Tom could hear it barking from faraway. Another dog joined that one, and then Tom saw the herder.

For a moment, he stood there, wondering whether the herder would be a friend or enemy. He couldn't be an enemy, because he couldn't have heard about the jailbreak. Could he be a friend?

With rubbery legs, Shannon started down the long hill. He walked, slid on the seat of his pants, walked. Halfway down he felt so weak that he had to stop and rest. He could see the herder clearly now, and he had a long, bushy beard and a floppy hat. Was he the one who had been about to be kicked to pieces in the Salty Dog that night? Could be. Tom got up and went on, sliding and walking.

The dogs saw him first and ran at him barking. He stood his ground and let them come. There were two of them, and they circled him, barking, but not threatening to bite. Sure. He had heard that while cow dogs were taught to bite but not bark, sheep dogs were taught to bark but not bite. He knew from experience that a range cow would fight a barking dog. Sheep ran from them. A yell from the herder pulled the dogs away from Tom. He didn't know whether to move forward or not.

The herder was carrying a rifle, and was no doubt wary of strangers. So he stood there until the herder waved to him, motioning him forward. Soon the two men were only a few yards apart. The dogs were watching Tom but making no moves toward him.

The herder grinned inside his beard, then frowned. "What the hairy hell happened to you?"

"Well, uh, I..." Tom tried to think of a believable lie, couldn't.

He could only hope the herder hadn't heard of the jailbreak.

"Get thrown off your horse?"

"Yeah, uh, I'm afoot and hungry as a pet bear."

"You're the one that pulled that young rooster off of me at Fortune, ain't you?"

"Yeah. Maybe you don't know it, but that started something that isn't finished yet."

The herder squinted at him, trying to figure out what he was talking about. He said, "Hungry, huh?"

"Yeah."

"Well, come on over to the wagon."

Not until then did Tom notice the camp wagon behind a clump of aspens. It had a canvas top with a stovepipe sticking out one end. The herder led the way and Tom followed on rubbery legs.

"When was the last time you ate?"

He managed a weak grin. "So long ago I don't remember." He decided not to mention the raven.

"I about starved once, and I know how it feels. Come on in."

The wagon had a canvas door on the side, and Tom followed the herder up the wooden steps and inside. There were a tarp-covered bed on a narrow cot, a one-burner cook-stove, a chair, a table about the size of a saddle blanket, and two wooden boxes. Both contained groceries.

"Best thing in the world for you right now is some buckskin stew. Shot a young bull elk couple days ago, and got some stew already cooked. Won't take long to get a fire going and heat it up." The herder opened the one-burner, put some small sticks in it, and struck a match.

Tom tried to make conversation. "Bet it takes a while to cook a stew at this altitude."

"All day, and then it doesn't taste right till it jells overnight. Sit down. I don't get much company and sometimes I forget my manners. Make yourself at home."

Shannon sat in the wooden chair, happy to be off his feet.

"Walked far?"

"Yeah." He knew the herder wanted to know more but wouldn't push him for it.

"Care for a smoke?" The herder pulled a long-stemmed pipe out of the pocket on the bib of his overalls. He produced a thin can of tobacco from a hip pocket.

"No thanks. I've got some makin's, but I don't feel much like smoking right now."

"I wouldn't either if I hadn't ate for a while." He uncovered a cast-iron pot, sniffed its contents, and put it on the stove. "Won't take long. That hurting you?" The old man was looking at the spot of blood on Tom's left side.

"Not much. Just got scratched."

"Bleeding. Got a bottle of whiskey here. Whiskey's got alcohol in it and it's not bad for cleaning a bleeding wound."

Tom knew he had to do something about that gash in his side. He wondered whether the herder would recognize it as a bullet wound. Maybe not. "Yeah, I guess I ought to clean it the best I can."

A whiskey bottle nearly full was produced from one of the wooden boxes, and Tom raised his shirttail, turned his back to the old man, and used his fingers to daub some whiskey on his wound. It burned like hell.

"Better give it a good soaking," the herder said. "Hell of a way to treat good whiskey," Tom said, grinning. He did the best he could with his fingers and tucked his shirttail back in.

They were silent while the wood fire warmed the iron pot. The herder acted as though he wanted to say more but didn't know what to say. Tom just plain didn't feel like talking. When the old man lifted the lid from the pot, he said, "It's warm enough." He took a tin plate from one of the boxes, ladled it full of stew, and handed it to Tom. It smelled delicious. Tom could see chunks of meat, potatoes, and turnips swimming in a thick gravy. He was handed a fork. "Dig in. I ate 'bout an hour ago and I ain't hungry now."

Tom took a bite. The meat was tender and good. He chewed and swallowed, hoping his stomach would behave.

"Man gets too hungry it's hard to eat sometimes. If you can't handle the meat, just sip the soup."

Grinning weakly, Tom said, "I think I can handle it. Wish I could cook like this." He ate slowly and chewed thoroughly. His stomach was glad to get it. Soon he cleaned his plate.

"Want some more?"

"No thanks. Sure was good."

"It's kinda like being too long without water. Drink too much at once and it can make you sick. Wait a few hours, and after I get my animals penned, we'll eat up what's left."

"I sure appreciate it."

"Go ahead and lay down on my bed if you want. I got to go keep an eye on my herd. Go ahead. Pull off your boots and make yourself at home."

The herder ducked his head to get through the door, and he stomped down the steps. Tom pulled off his boots, sighed with relief, wiggled his toes inside his cotton socks, and lay back on the bed. Within ten minutes he was asleep.

CHAPTER 9

It was the smell of coffee that awakened him. For a few seconds he lay still, moving only his eyes, trying to figure out where he was. His eyes took in the wooden hoops overhead, which held the canvas top over the wagon, the stove, chair, the coffeepot on the stove. He was alone, and he sat up and hurriedly pulled on his boots. A fire was going in the stove and the coffeepot was boiling. Moving woodenly, Shannon pushed open the canvas door and looked outside.

The old sheepherder was squatted before an open fire, pushing something with a stick. He glanced up, saw Tom, and grinned, showing a gap in the front of his teeth. "Time to eat again. Got to make up for all those missed meals."

Tom came down the steps. "Anyone else here?"

"Naw. Nobody but me and my dogs." The dogs were sitting on the other side of the fire, watching Tom.

"Where are your sheep?"

"Yonder. I got a pen I made out of quaker poles. Keep 'em penned up at night. The dogs keep the coyotes away."

Tom squatted before the fire, and saw what the old man was doing. A dutch oven sat surrounded by hot coals, and inside was a batch of biscuits just beginning to brown. Nothing ever smelled better. The old man was poking at the coals.

"Does, uh, does anyone ever come here?"

The herder glanced at Tom and grinned. "Saw four men all summer. Two of them were Injuns. Saw a couple of bucks a while back. I watched them and they watched me and then they left, riding their ponies bareback. Came back that night and stole two of my sheep."

"Just the two bucks? That's all you saw?"

"Yeah. I figure they were hunting meat and decided to see what sheep tasted like. I had to stay up every night for a week after that, afraid they'd come back."

"Utes?"

"Reckon they were. I can't always tell one breed from another."

"Do you go to town often?"

"Naw. Once in a blue moon. Had to go that day to buy some coffee and tobacca and some flour and baking soda. It was a mistake to go in the saloon, but I figured a drink of whiskey wouldn't hurt nothing." He glanced again at Tom. "Trouble was, I didn't stop at one drink and I drank too much."

"Yeah, I heard you passed out at one of the tables and was there all night."

"Oughta have my ass kicked. Left my sheep in the pen and my dogs to watch them. If I'd have got shot or beat to death, the sheep would have starved."

He used an iron hook to lift the dutch oven out of the fire and place it on the bare ground.

"Yeah, I guess not many folks know where your camp is."

"That cowman knows. Saw some of his boys twice this summer."

"Wheeler?"

"Yeah. He always knows where I am."

"Did they bother you?"

"Naw. Didn't come over and be neighborly either. Don't like sheep, I reckon. Somebody told me you're a cowman."

"Oh, I've got a few cows. I've been making my living skidding logs and mucking in the mines."

"Good grazing country down there on the flats. Colder than the hubs of hell and the snow gets ass-deep sometimes, but most of the time the wind and the sun cleans the snow off the south slopes."

"I've been able to winter what few cattle I have down there."

"Time's coming when old Wheeler is going to claim it all. I

heard he's buying land from the government."

"Some day it'll all belong to whoever can buy it."

The herder touched one of the biscuits. "Time to eat. Can you stand some more of my stew? Got these to go with it."

"There's nothing I'd like better."

He was ashamed of himself the way he ate. Between the two of them they finished the stew and half the biscuits. But the herder was pleased. "Been a long time since I cooked for anybody. Good to see you putting it away."

"Have you always been a sheepman?"

That brought a scowl from the herder. He got up from the bunk he had been sitting on and poured a cup of coffee. "Help yourself to the java."

Tom poured himself a cup.

"Naw. I fought with the Union army. We were on opposite sides in the war. I heard you were a Johnny Reb."

"The war is over. There aren't supposed to be any sides now."

"That's the way I want it, but some folks think the fighting is still going on."

"It has to be over. That's all there is to it. The South will never be the same, but we can't spend the rest of our lives crying about it. We have to be one nation."

Blowing on his coffee to cool it, the herder said, "Yep."

They both sipped hot black coffee. The old man filled his pipe, tamped the tobacco in, and lit it. Tom rolled a cigarette and inhaled deeply.

"Came west to hunt for gold. Didn't find any. Met a man with a hundred sheep to sell. Bought them. Bought his wagon and his dogs. Fixing to move this bunch down to the flats in another week and stay the winter, and in the spring I'll be looking for a buyer."

"Getting out of the business, huh?"

"Yeah. Too lonely. I like it here in the mountains in the summer, but it's too lonely. I got to talking to myself too much. Even answer myself sometimes."

Grinning, Tom said, "I wouldn't like it, but I hear there's money in sheep."

"Hope to hell there is."

Outside, the wind had picked up and it sighed around the corners of the wagon. Tom wondered how much the old man knew about him. He knew he had been a Confederate soldier. He'd heard someone talk about him. Did he know he had been convicted of murder?

"Uh, did you say you passed out at the Salty Dog that night?"

"Yeah. I wasn't used to drinking. Time was when I could have drunk a lot more than that and gone on about my business."

"I'll bet you wasted no time getting out of town when you woke up."

"Shore didn't. I loaded my grub on a packhorse and got on my other horse and hightailed it for here."

"You've got horses?"

"Yep. Two of them. I can ride them or work them in harness. Got them staked out over yonder."

"I don't suppose you'd care to sell one."

"Wish I could help you there, but I need them."

"Yeah." Tom took a puff of his cigarette. "Uh, before you passed out, did you see or hear anything in the Salty Dog—I mean, anything that was unusual? After I left, I mean."

"Naw. Can't say I did. Seemed pretty quiet after you left."

"Nothing happened then? That kid, Scott Wheeler, did he get into it with anyone else?"

"Don't think so. He didn't bother me no more."

"Did he stay very long?"

"Weel"—the herder pulled at his beard—"if I recollect right, he stayed a while and played faro or blackjack with that dandy dealer. Most everybody else was playing poker at a table in the back."

"Did you know that Scott Wheeler was murdered that night?"

"What?" The herder was lifting his coffee cup to his mouth, and he stopped with his hand in midair.

"Yeah. That's why I'm asking so many questions."

"Are you telling me..." He took another sip of his coffee. "Are you telling me that you were accused of killing him?"

"Yeah." There, it was out. Tom wondered if he had made a mistake.

"That's why you're afoot and half-starved. You ran away from

54

them."

"Yeah." He studied the old man's face, trying to decide whether he had made a mistake.

The old man stared hard at him, then shook his head. "You don't strike me as a killer."

"I'm not. I never killed anyone except in the war. But it seems like I'm the only one who got into a fight with Scott Wheeler."

Silence. The herder smoked his pipe. Tom sipped coffee and looked around for a place to snub out his cigarette. The wind moaned outside and it was getting dark. The herder got up and lit a lamp. "Toss it in the stove there."

Shannon took the lid lifter, opened the stove lid, and dropped his cigarette butt in the fire. "I told you about it because someone might come along and ask if you saw me."

"I didn't see you."

"I appreciate that. You might have saved my life. I was so damn tired and sick when I came down here, I'm not sure I could have gone much farther."

"You might have saved my life too."

"I'll go. I don't want to get you in trouble with the law."

"Wait till morning. You need some rest."

Tom pondered that. "I'll leave early in the morning." He rolled another cigarette. "You say Wheeler didn't get into any more trouble that night. Did he do anything but play faro?"

"Not that I saw. He was playing with that dealer, that dandy with the slick hair and all. They were playing with two others for a while, then those two left and it was just the kid and the dealer."

"And that's all that happened?"

"That's all I saw."

"Damn," Tom muttered. "Someone wanted Wheeler dead. I sure wish I knew who." He studied his cigarette. "What was Zack Parmell doing? You know, the foreman at the Running W."

"He was in the poker game that was going on."

Tom shook his head sadly. "There's more to this. I wish I knew what."

"Only thing happened is some gent came in while that kid and that dandy were playing faro and whispered something to the dandy."

"Yeah? That's all?"

"That's all. Pretty soon after that the kid quit playing. He went to the bar and had a drink, and that's the last I recollect."

Shannon smoked another cigarette, and the old man invited him to sleep in the one bed. "I can take a couple of blankets and sleep with my dogs."

"Oh no, I don't want to take your bed."

"Go ahead. You need some rest. When you leave here you'll have to leave walking."

"No, I'll sleep on the ground."

"Naw, you take the bed."

No feather bed would have been more comfortable. Tom slept until daylight and again was awakened by the smell of coffee. It worried him that he had slept while the old man came in, started a fire in the stove, and put the coffee on. A man running from the law had to be more careful than that.

He went to the creek and washed his face. When the water settled, he saw his reflection and saw he was growing a beard. He had never grown a beard, but decided it might help disguise him. Back inside the camp wagon he watched the herder unwrap a piece of blanket from around a crock, lift out the dough inside the crock, and lay it on the table. Shannon could smell the fermentation, and knew it was sourdough. The herder mixed flour and baking soda with it and tossed it a small piece at a time onto a flat skillet.

They ate thick-sliced bacon and sourdough hotcakes covered with molasses and drank black coffee. The meal over, Tom gathered his two guns and prepared to leave.

"It's three days' walk that way." The old man pointed southeast. "I'll give you a blanket and some grub."

"Are you sure you can spare it?"

"Yep."

He sliced some bacon off a slab, took a paper bag of dried fruit, and put it all on top of a rose-colored blanket he had spread over the bed. He rolled up the blanket, tied the ends together with a piece of heavy twine, and handed it to Tom. "You can carry this over your shoulder. Here, take some matches. I'll clean up every trace so nobody will know you've been here. That is, if anybody comes.

Doubt if they will."

It was time to go. Shannon stuck out his hand and they shook. "Here's wishing you a good winter."

"You too."

He walked away. When he got to the top of the ridge he stopped, looked back and said to himself, "I don't even know his name."

CHAPTER 10

It took all day to get to the Ute Trail road, walking, climbing, sliding. The road wound like a pink ribbon over the low hills, around the high hills, and out of sight over the horizon. The sun was sitting on the western ridge when Tom dropped his bundle and sat on a rock at the edge of the road.

He would have been surprised to see a wagon coming this time of day, and he picked out a spot near a trickle of a stream and under some ponderosas a hundred yards from the road, and made his camp. Using his butcher knife, he cut a green, sappy branch off one of the trees and used that to hold his bacon strips over an open fire. When the ends curled he laid them on a rock, and while they cooled he ate a double handful of dried fruit. His meal over, he smoked and wondered what lay ahead. He thought about Mary.

What was she doing? Still working at the Silver Lode Cafe? Still reading by lamplight at night? Would she try again to sell her house and leave Fortune, or would she wait there, hoping to hear from him? He would write her a letter and mail it from the next settlement and again urge her to leave Fortune and go back to her hometown in Iowa. Fortune was no place for a lady. Hell—Tom frowned—Fortune was no place for anyone. And waiting for him was useless. He would always be a fugitive and he wouldn't ask—wouldn't even allow—her to live with the fear of being caught. But thinking of Mary caused an ache in his chest that wouldn't go away. Mary, with the wide gray eyes, the trim waist and ankles, the neat brown hair. Widowed at twenty-seven. Her husband, a miner, had left her a frame house in the lawless town of Fortune and little else. Why had she stayed?

The reason she gave seemed logical. She had tried to sell the house her husband had left her, but got no takers. People were becoming afraid to live in Fortune and were leaving. A house and lot were worth next to nothing. Mary had said she couldn't just give away the house her husband had built for her. But Shannon hoped she wouldn't be so stubborn as to further endanger her life.

She was a bright young woman. Read everything she could get her hands on, and knew more about the world than most folks. A good woman. Good at asking questions, and knew more about Tom Shannon than he knew about himself. Mary, Mary. Tom shook his head sadly. He would never forget her.

Grateful for the blanket, he rolled up in it under the trees and slept. Twice during the night he got up and put more wood on the fire, but at daylight the fire had gone out anyway. He rebuilt it and had a breakfast of the bacon and more dried fruit. No coffee, but then, he thought with a wry grin, a man couldn't have everything. With his blanket rolled up and hung from his shoulder again, Tom went to the road and resumed walking, heading east.

Walking on the road was easier than walking cross-country, and he stepped right along, figuring it would take two more days to get to the town of Tarryall. He kept looking behind him, not wanting anyone coming from the west to see him, recognize him. It wasn't until shortly before noon that he saw a wagon.

Quickly, he ducked out of sight behind a grove of aspens, where he lay on his stomach and waited for the wagon to pass. It was a freight wagon pulled by four horses, no doubt going to one of the cities on the eastern slopes of the Rockies for supplies. Ten minutes later another freight wagon went by, also heading east. When they were out of sight, he walked on.

About midafternoon he hailed a wagon coming from the east and heading toward Fortune. A man and woman shared the wooden seat behind two mules, and two small boys in ragged overalls looked over the edge of the wagon box at him.

The man, a grizzled, middle-aged gent in a wide hat, kept his finger on the trigger of a Henry rifle as he "Whoaed" his team. Tom held his rifle by the barrel across his shoulder, a position he hoped would indicate he had no intention of using it.

"I'm walking to the next town—what is it? Tarryall?—and I was hoping you could sell me some grub."

"Ain't got none to spare, mister. Just enough for me and the woman and kids."

"Oh. Well then, I wish you luck."

"You plumb out?"

"Not plumb out, but not enough for more than two skinny meals."

"Wal, I reckon we can spare some salted sowbelly. Can we git grub and stuff at Fortune?"

"Yeah. There's a mercantile there. If you can spare some, I'll pay you for it and you can buy more at Fortune."

"Wal, I reckon it'll be all right."

"You got somethin' to boil it in?" The woman spoke for the first time. She had a lean, wrinkled face and a thin willowy body. Her hair was covered by a green satin cloth.

"No, ma'am, I haven't."

"Give 'im that little tin pot, John. Nobody can eat salted sowbelly without boilin' it."

The man stepped to the rear of the wagon and opened a wooden keg. He reached in and pulled out a slab of meat, handed it down to Tom.

"How much do I owe you?"

"Oh, I dunno. What do you think, Mabel?"

"How come you're walkin'?" the woman asked.

"Lost my horse."

"Well, if you've got money well take a dollar. If you ain't got no money you don't owe us nothin'." Tom turned his back to them as he peeled two bills off the roll he carried in his pocket. "Here's two dollars, and I sure am obliged."

"How much farther to Fortune?"

"Three days, I'd guess. You prospecting?"

"Naw. Got a job in the sawmill."

"Good luck."

"You too, mister," the woman said.

The two kids stared wide-eyed at him as the man clucked to the team and the wagon rolled on down the road.

That was the last wagon Shannon saw that day. Another night eating the bacon and dried fruit, sleeping on the ground. Next morning he filled the small tin pot with water and got the water boiling, then dropped in the sowbelly. He let it boil for ten minutes, pulled it out, and placed it on a rock to cool. Most of the salt had come out in the boiling water, but the meat still was too salty to eat. He ate a thick slice of it anyway.

He saw two more wagons that day, but didn't try to stop them. At dusk he topped a hill and saw a house below. It was a clapboard house, and there was a barn and some corrals. Two toilets stood behind the house. It had to be a stage stop. A place for a change of horses and a place where passengers could get out, stretch their legs, and relieve themselves. It was a place Tom had to avoid.

Stage drivers carried news.

He found another camp spot out of sight of the road and the buildings. He ate the rest of his bacon and dried fruit, then went back to the top of the hill and watched lights come on in the house below. Dim lamplights. In the morning he boiled the sowbelly again and let it boil for about twenty minutes. It wasn't as salty now, but still salty. Tom washed it down with water from a creek, and was grateful for being in the mountains where there was always a creek not too far away.

The country below the stage stop wasn't as hilly, and he realized there was no place to hide if a stage came rocking along. He set out again, keeping to a course that paralleled the road. The next vehicle he saw was a freight wagon coming from Fortune, and then he saw the stage. He remembered that the stage traveled from Fairplay to the east twice each week. It was pulled by a four-horse team, and the driver changed horses every fifteen or twenty miles, depending on the terrain.

He lay in a gully until the stage passed, then got up and went on. He kept going, even after dusk, hoping to reach Tarryall and spend the night in a hotel. Two hours after dark he saw lights again. A lot of lights.

A town.

* * *

Going into the town could be dangerous. The news could have spread about a condemned man breaking out of jail and running on foot. But Tom Shannon couldn't walk forever. He had to get into town, buy a horse and saddle, buy a meal, some groceries, buy some clean clothes. He decided he wouldn't stay there any longer than he had to, and that then he would be on his way east to Colorado City.

It was a dark night, and only dim lights illuminated the glass windows of Tarryall. Tom trudged down the main street and looked for a hotel sign. He passed a pedestrian, a bearded man in jackboots and suspenders. They said, "Howdy" to each other. There wasn't much traffic on the street and plankwalks.

He found a hotel sign hanging from a roof that stretched over the sidewalk. It was a two-story building. Wishing he weren't so rangy-looking, but knowing there was nothing he could do about it, he stepped through an open door into a lamp-lite lobby.

There were two wooden chairs, a wooden floor, and a wooden desk with a row of keys hanging from wooden pegs beside it. A small bell sat on the desk. Tom picked it up and shook it. A little man with a bald head, striped shirt, and sleeve garters came out of a room behind the desk.

Shannon forced himself to smile, trying to look like a man who had nothing to worry about. "Sure hope you've got a vacant room. Lost my horse and I must have walked ten miles."

The little man looked him over briefly and said, "Six bits. If you want a bath it's a dollar."

"I sure do need a bath. Is there a place to eat in town?"

"Tarryall Cafe. Across the street and down the block that way." He pointed east. "Closes pretty soon."

"Thanks. I'll just put this blanket in my room and get right over there."

Small room upstairs. Narrow brass bedstead with a thin mattress, muslin sheets, and two cotton blankets. A washstand with a basin and a pitcher of water sat beside a scarred chiffonier. Over that was a cracked mirror a foot square. Pegs to hang his clothes on. He looked at himself in the mirror and was glad Mary couldn't see him.

His eyes had a hollow, haunted look, his face was grimy, and his beard was two inches long.

Bathroom downstairs, he'd been told.

Fine. But first he'd better get over to that cafe. He dropped his blanket roll on the floor and went back down to the street. There were horsemen on the street now, and a few pedestrians on the plankwalk. A few stared curiously at him, but their faces showed no recognition. Inside the Tarryall Cafe he found four tables covered with red-checkered oilcloth and a wooden counter with stools. He sat on a stool before a plump young woman who had her hair pulled back in a bun. Not pretty like Mary. He was the only customer. "Roast beef and boiled potatoes and gravy," she said.

He forced himself to smile again. "Coffee too? I sure could use some coffee."

"Yeah." Her eyes narrowed. "Traveling through? I never seen you before."

"Yes, ma'am. I'm on my way to Fortune, but I lost my horse. Just let him break his hobbles and run off. If I can't find him I'll have to buy another."

"See Ben Stumps at that barn at the end of the street. He's always ready to sell or trade or buy horses."

"Thanks. I'll do that."

He had to ring the bell again to fetch the hotel manager and ask where to get water for a bath. The bathroom, he discovered, had a long tin tub, but no water.

"Have to heat some on the stove," the little bald man said.

"I'll be in my room. Call me when the water is ready. Sure do need a bath."

The water was only lukewarm and there wasn't much of it, about two bucketful. But he managed to scrub himself down, and when he got out of the tub he felt better. The wound in his left side was still raw, and he knew he'd have to attend to it as soon as possible. It didn't hurt anymore except when he tried to raise his left arm over his head. When he crawled into bed he remembered it had been over two years since he'd slept in a hotel. That was at Pueblo, a town east of the mountains on the Arkansas River. He'd bought his cattle in Pueblo and had driven them ahead of him as he traveled west to Fortune.

Sleep came easily, but he woke up with a start around midnight when he heard boots clomping up the stairs. He lay awake, tense, muscles bunched until the footsteps went past his door. Lord, he thought, he had to get out of this part of the country, all the way to the eastern slopes. Colorado City. Maybe even Denver. He had to get out of Tarryall as soon as possible.

CHAPTER 11

For a few seconds, while he was at breakfast in the Tarryall Cafe, he wished he hadn't left his guns in the hotel room. The cafe was crowded and there was only one vacant stool at the counter. He was stuffing himself with bacon, hotcakes, and coffee when he saw the plump young woman point him out to a tall man with a walrus moustache and a pistol on his right hip. The man walked directly at him.

Shannon had an urge to run. He calculated the distance to the door and wondered if he could get out the door and around the corner without being stopped by a bullet in the back.

He stood up, ready.

"You the feller that wants to buy a horse?" The tall man was talking to him.

"Well, uh, yeah." He couldn't help letting his breath out with a grunt as he sat again.

"I'm Ben Stumps. I got all sizes and colors."

"Well, uh, as soon as I finish my coffee I'll look at them."

The tall man stood beside him. "Joannie tells me your horse got away from you. Broke his hobbles, or something. What does he look like?"

"Oh, he's a bay, about a thousand pounds. Got black legs and a white spot about the size of a double eagle between his eyes. Short back." Tom was surprised at how easily the lie came.

"I'll ask around. He might show up somewhere."

"Trouble is, I've got to get on my way. I've got to buy another horse."

"Where you headed?"

"Over to Fortune. Got a job riding for the Running W."

"That the outfit that had some cattle stolen a few days ago?"

"Why, I don't know. I never heard."

"Yeah. Feller came through town in a wagon with his family and said he was leaving Fortune. Said the thieves are so thick you can't look up without being robbed. Said the Running W lost about eighty head to the thieves."

Tom swallowed a lump in his throat and took a sip of coffee to hide what was going through his mind. He believed he would recognize one of the rustlers if he saw him. And the dead man he'd left back there had no doubt been supposed to help with the rustling. He wondered if some of his cattle were among those stolen. He drained his coffee cup, stood, and paid for his meal. The tall man stepped back to allow him to pass.

"Come on over to the barn and pick out a good horse. I'll give you a fair shake."

"I need a good-sized one," Tom said as they peered between the poles of a pole corral. "He's got to carry me and some grub and blankets."

"See that sorrel over there? The one with the stocking legs? He'll go about twelve hundred pounds and he can carry anything."

"Doesn't look like he could run."

"Wal, he's no racehorse, but he's a stout old pony, and he won't run off and leave you afoot. He's been hobbled and he's been staked out. He's so gentle I could crawl under him if I wanted to. Don't want to, howsomever. And I had him shod last week."

Tom crawled between the poles and went over to the horse. The animal stood and waited for him.

"See. You can catch him anywhere."

Tom ran his hands down the horse's legs, looking for splints. He pried its mouth open and looked at the teeth. He could tell by the angle of the teeth that the horse was not young.

"How old did you say he is?"

"Nine years old."

Shannon flashed a grin. Most men couldn't tell a horse's age beyond the age of nine, but he had planned to make a career of raising good horses back in Kentucky. Before the war, that is. "Smooth in the lowers. Twelve, I'd say."

"Got a lot of good years left in him."

"How much are you asking?"

"Hundred. He's worth more, but I've got more horses than I can feed."

"Give you sixty. That is, if he doesn't throw me off."

"Nope. Eighty-five and not a cent less."

"Sixty-five and not a cent more."

"Seventy-five."

"All right. Now, have you got a used saddle for sale?"

He bought the horse and an old A-fork saddle that wouldn't have held together if he'd roped a cow from it, but was all right for just riding. Next, he went to a general store two doors down from the hotel and bought a change of clothes, including a blanket-lined jacket, tobacco, groceries, a small iron skillet, a canvas tent half, forty feet of grass rope, and a belt holster and a saddle scabbard for his guns.

At Ben Stumps's barn he rolled everything inside the tent half and tied it behind the cantle of the old saddle. He was ready to leave when a wagon pulled by two tired horses came up. One of the horses was limping badly on its left forefoot. "Howdy," said Ben Stumps, looking over the horses.

A man in bib overalls, a checkered shirt, and floppy hat climbed down from the seat. A woman in a wool pullover cap and a shapeless gingham dress stayed on the seat. "Got a lame horse," the man said. "He's sound, but he's got a rock bruise. Got anything to trade for?"

"Shore. Horse tradin's my middle name. Where you coming from?"

"Fortune. Had to get out of there. A gang of robbers and killers're takin over the town."

"Yeah, that's what I heard."

"Ain't safe. They shot the deputy four days ago. Killed 'im. I been workin' a claim and findin' some yaller, but ever' time I got a poke full somebody stuck a shotgun at my head and took it away from me. They'll even rob women. Threatened to shoot my wife once if she didn't tell 'em where I hid my dust. They rob ever'thing and ever'body. Allus wear them black rags over their faces so you don't know who they are."

"Killed the deputy, you say?" Ben Stumps shook his head. Tom was listening.

"Yup. Ain't got no law over there no more. Nobody wants the job. Ain't nobody safe."

"Wal, I'll be damned," Ben Stumps said. "Soon's I take care of some business, I'll take a look at that lame horse and make a trade with you."

Picking up his reins, Tom started to put his foot in the stirrup and mount, then stopped when he heard Ben Stumps say, "Just hold it right there, Tom Shannon."

"What?" Shannon turned and saw the tall man standing behind him, pointing a six-gun at him. He didn't have to feign surprise. He was surprised. Until now, no one had seemed suspicious. "You're him, all right. We got word about you."

"Well..." Tom stammered, "Who are you? Are you the law?"

"Yup. Deputy Holeman ain't here right now; and I'm in charge. I'm locking you up and sending a message to Fortune."

"But..." Tom was still at a loss for words.

"That story about your horse running off, that was just a tall tale. You're Tom Shannon and you broke jail over to Fortune and you walked here or bummed a ride in a wagon. You're him, all right."

"But why did you sell me a horse and saddle?" Then Tom knew the answer to his own question.

Ben Stumps had his money and would keep it, and he would keep the horse and saddle too.

"Just stand mighty still. Don't move a hair. This old forty-four'll blow a hole in you I can put my fist through."

CHAPTER 12

Tom didn't move when Ben Stumps took the pistol from his new belt holster.

"Now march. We got a lockup."

The man in overalls was watching and listening with his mouth open. He turned to his wife. "He's the one, ain't he, Ruthie? He's the one broke jail. He was gonna hang for shootin' a man in the back. I almost didn't rec'nize him with that beard and all, but he's the one, ain't he?"

The woman spoke without emotion. "I don't know. I never seen him."

"March, mister." Ben Stumps's pistol was printed at Tom's middle. "That way."

Moving stiffly, Shannon walked. Silently, he cursed himself. He should have been more careful. Should have— Aw, what's the use thinking about what he should have done? He had had to stop in Tarryall. Had needed to buy a horse and grub. He'd known he was taking a chance, but he'd had no choice. Now he was back where he'd started. He would be locked up again and kept locked up until someone from Fortune came for him. Who would come? Deputy Atwell was dead, and no one wanted his job. Someone would come, and he'd be taken back in a wagon, tied hand and foot, and he'd be hanged.

He walked with wooden steps, Ben Stumps right behind him. On the sidewalk, they passed two men in miners' clothes who noticed

69

the gun in Stumps's hand and asked, "What's goin' on, Ben?"

"Got a jailbreaker here. They were gonna hang him over at Fortune and he busted out."

"What's he done?"

"Killed a man. Shot him in the back from a dark alley."

"Oughta hang 'im. If they don't, we oughta."

"One way or another, he's gonna get hung."

Tom kept walking. Other townspeople saw what was happening and stared.

"Right here," Stumps said.

They were in front of a frame building with the words United States Deputy Marshal painted in white letters on a window. "In there."

Tom went through the door. The deputy's office was almost a duplicate of the one in Fortune. Wood-frame front, but with a connecting jail made of heavy timbers. A desk and wooden chair in one corner and a gun rack on a wall over the desk. Wanted posters on another wall. Tom's name was not on any of the posters.

"Now," Stumps said, "I want you to lean over and put your hands on top of that desk. And spread your feet. I'm holding this forty-four right where I couldn't miss if I wanted to, and I'm gonna take ever'thing out of your pockets."

They were alone in the room.

"Do what I said, God damn it. I oughta make you strip naked. Make sure you're not hiding a boot gun or something."

Shannon put his hands on the desk. He had to lean over to do it.

"Spread them feet."

He did.

A rough hand went through his pockets while the bore of the forty-four kept a steady pressure against his back. His roll of money was taken from a pants pocket and put on the desk. "Bet you stole it," Stumps grunted. Tobacco and cigarette papers were taken from a shirt pocket. There was nothing else.

"Now, sit down on the floor and take off them boots." Stumps stepped back, but kept the six-gun level.

"What are you going to do with my money?"

"Never mind."

Sarcasm and bitterness swept over Tom. "Bet you'll keep it. Just like you'll keep the money I paid you for a horse and saddle."

"You calling me a thief?"

Tom hesitated. It was foolish to anger the man. He could be shot right here. Ben Stumps could kill him and say it was self-defense. He would be a minor hero for shooting an escaped killer. But dammit, Tom was angry. He was no thief. Ben Stumps was. He was stealing from him at the point of a gun and he would get by with it.

"Yeah," he hissed, "you're a thief. You're using the law to steal. You're the worst kind of thief."

He saw the blow coming. Not in time to dodge it, but in time to roll with it. Still, bright lights shot through his brain as the gun in Ben Stumps's hand whipped up and thudded against the side of his head. He staggered back and almost fell.

"You wanta call me that again?"

He shook his head, trying to clear his vision. He steadied himself, planted his feet, and said, "Yeah, you're a goddam thief."

This time he was ready. When the blow started, his left hand shot up and got hold of the gun. His other hand came up and got hold of Stumps's right wrist. Using his hip for a fulcrum, he spun the tall man around and slammed him against the desk, then swung his right elbow back and pounded him in the face with it.

Keeping his hold on the gun, he hit Stumps twice in the face with his elbow. Again. Stumps yelled, but his voice choked off as Tom hit him a fourth time, this time in the throat.

Now Tom was holding Stumps's gun arm over the edge of the desk, pushing down. His teeth were bared in a grimace as he bore down—a desperate grimace. Stumps grunted and tried to holler again. Another blow from Tom's elbow again cut it off.

The two men grunted and strained, but Stumps was gagging from the blow to the throat and was weakening. Finally his fingers on the gun relaxed and Shannon jerked it out of his hand.

Spinning, he slammed the gun against the side of the tall man's head, then stepped back and let him fall.

Tom glanced around hurriedly. He was surprised that no one had shown up in the doorway yet. Was there a jail key? Yeah, there it was on a ring, hanging from a nail in the wall.

Moving fast, Shannon grabbed the key, opened the connecting door to the jail, saw the cell door was open, went back to Stumps and grabbed him by the belt and shirt collar. The man was big and heavy, and Tom had to strain to drag him through the connecting door and into the cell.

Breathing hard from the exertion, he shut the cell door and locked it. He went back to the desk, put his money and tobacco in his pocket and his gun in its brand-new holster. He picked up his hat and looked for another way out of the building.

Whoever built the jail at Fortune had to have built this one too, because it had the same kind of heavy iron sliding latch on the back door, the kind that could be opened only from the inside. Shannon slid the latch back, cracked the door open, and looked out into an alley. A saddle horse was tied to a hitching post fifty feet away, but there was no human in sight.

All right, calm down, he told himself. Walk out like nothing happened. He rubbed a palm over the side of his head where he had been hit with a gun barrel and put the hat on. He had to tip it to one side a little, at a cocky angle, to keep it off the sore spot.

Now just walk out. Calm. Like a man taking a leisurely stroll.

CHAPTER 13

He felt like running. His nerves screamed at him to run. But he ordered his feet to move slowly, casually. He discovered he was carrying the jail key, and quickly he put it in his hip pocket. Walk easy. Like everything was right in the world. Easy.

Two men were unloading a freight wagon behind the general store, but they didn't look his way. A cowboy untied the saddle horse, mounted, and rode past Tom. "Mornin'," he said, and went on.

Tom's head hurt and his right elbow—the one he had used to batter Ben Stumps's face—was numb. Walk easy.

The horse he had bought was still there in front of the barn, still saddled. The team of horses from Fortune had been unhitched and were standing with the harness on tied to the side of the wagon. A teenaged boy with hair the color of straw was raking manure out of a barn stall. No one else was in sight.

Tom mounted the horse and rode out of town at a slow trot, going east. He expected to hear a shout and gunfire from behind him. He expected to hear hoofbeats. No one paid him any attention. He willed himself not to look back.

On the outskirts of town he urged the horse into a faster trot. A horseman riding at a trot drew no attention from anyone. He passed two other riders and a man driving a buggy. They only nodded at him. He rode at a trot for two miles, then, when he was away from all the houses and all the stacked lumber, he booted the horse into a gallop, still going east.

Keeping the horse on a lope, Tom began looking for two things: first, he wanted to pass someone else heading for Tarryall, and second, he wanted to find a ravine or a line of willows or something he could hide behind going north.

The horse was getting winded from running when he saw a light spring wagon coming toward him. He kept the horse on a lope until he passed the wagon and was out of sight of it. Then he allowed the animal to slow to a walk.

Now he had been seen. The man and woman in the wagon would tell his pursuers he was heading east at a gallop. His pursuers—and there would be some sooner or later—would run their mounts half to death trying to catch up with him.

As soon as his horse caught its wind, he urged it into a trot again, looking to the north. After another mile he saw what he was looking for—a shallow, heavily timbered valley between two hills. He reined his horse in that direction and kept at a trot until he was in the timber out of sight of the road.

About a mile from the road the terrain slanted upward into the high hills. Allowing his mount to walk now, he kept going north until he knew he was far from the town of Tarryall, then he turned west. There, under a timbered hill, he dismounted, loosened the saddle cinch, and let the horse rest.

They would be convinced he was heading east for Colorado City as fast as his horse could carry him. They would never suspect he was going back to Fortune, the town he had just run from. They—a posse—would include Ben Stumps as soon as they could get him out of his own jail. Tom grinned when he thought about it. He had the key. In fact, he still had it in his hip pocket. Remembering that, he threw the key into the brown leaves under a clump of aspens. They would have to take the heavy bolts out of the cell door to free Stumps, and that would take time.

Wouldn't that thieving horse trader be mad, though? He'd be so mad he'd kill Tom on sight if he had a chance. He'd have to. The last thing he'd want was for Tom to tell everyone about his thieving ways and how easy it had been to get away from him. Tom chuckled to himself. Wonder what kind of wild tale old Stumps is telling. Though his head ached, his right elbow was back to normal now. He bent and

74

straightened the elbow several times to be sure of that.

He tightened the cinch on his newly purchased saddle and rode on, going west. An hour later he topped a high hill, stopped, and looked down on the town of Tarryall far in the distance. There were three mine headframes south of town and another long sheet-metal building with a tall smokestack. A mining town, he surmised. A stopping place for travelers. A place to buy supplies.

That's what Fortune was too. Was. Now it was being deserted. No one was safe there, travelers had said. Mary wasn't safe. He rolled a cigarette, struck a match on the rawhide-covered horn of the saddle, and lit it. Mary owned a house that she was reluctant to abandon. Another woman shared the house with her and paid rent, but would the other woman stay? Would Mary be alone in the house? Tom knew that if he wrote Mary a letter, she would meet him anywhere, but he didn't want her to do that. Yet she was in danger where she was. She needed a man. She needed him.

The cigarette tasted good, and he drew deeply on it. He wouldn't dare show himself in Fortune. If the townsmen were looking for blood when he ran, they would be even more bloodthirsty now that Deputy Atwell had been murdered. Or was everyone cowed and ready to leave? Judging from what he'd heard, a gang of robbers and killers were running the town of Fortune now, the same gang that had been terrorizing the South Park country for six or eight months.

Tom Shannon smoked, a worry frown between his eyes. He stubbed out the cigarette on the saddlehorn and touched the horse's sides with his boot heels.

He was going back.

CHAPTER 14

He rode at a trot most of the time. Only on the steep hills did he allow the horse to slow to a walk. After about twenty miles he got back on the Ute Trail road. It was either follow the road or climb steep hills on either side of the road.

Twice he passed wagons going east, away from Fortune, and one of them carried a family, furniture and all. Shannon hailed them, but they wore pinched expressions on their faces and were obviously afraid that he was part of a gang intent on robbing them. When he saw the effect he was having on the family, he touched his hat brim, said, "Howdy folks," and rode on.

The sky was clear now and the sun warmed up the world he was in, and Tom had hopes that a long, warm fall season was ahead. Late in the day he looked for a place to spend the night, and found a grassy spot near a creek, a place where his new mount could graze. He off-saddled, and tied the end of his new rope to a halter on the horse, and let the animal drink out of the creek, then crop the tall country grass. Instead of tying the other end of the rope to a rock, Tom held it and watched. He had to find out what the horse would do if it got the rope between its feet and got tangled in it. Most horses would panic and injure themselves trying to get loose unless they were accustomed to being staked out. Shannon watched and twice flipped the rope up between the horse's hind legs. It merely stepped over the rope and went on grazing.

A good horse for the work he had.

The mountain grass was strong feed, and the horse was feeling good when Tom saddled up next morning and resumed his journey. The sore spot on the side of his head where he had been hit with a gun barrel was slightly swollen, and he had to continue wearing his hat in a cocky, rakish fashion.

At midmorning he met a string of five freight wagons leaving Fortune, and he rode alongside the lead wagon a short distance and talked with the driver. The wagons belonged to a merchant in Fortune and were going all the way to Colorado City for supplies, a two-week round trip. Yes, he was told, a gang of killers and robbers were making life hazardous in that part of the country, but they had not bothered the merchants. The driver's eyes narrowed as he stared at Tom, but if he recognized him he didn't say so. Yes, Deputy Atwell had been killed, shot from ambush, and no, the town had no law enforcement officer. Marshal George Bennett had come from Fairplay to try to hire another deputy, but everyone was afraid to take the job.

Tom reined his horse to the side of the road and waited there until the last of the wagons had gone by. If he was recognized, no one wanted to make an issue of it.

He camped again an hour before dark, wanting to give his horse plenty of time to eat and rest. It would take a grazing horse several hours to eat its fill, he knew, and it would continue grazing after dark. But it needed time to rest too. He fried some bacon, ate a can of beans, smoked, and tried to figure out what to do and how to do it. Fortune was less than a day's journey ahead for a man on a strong, healthy horse, and he needed a plan. He couldn't just ride into town in the daylight. He'd have to sneak around in the dark.

Mary wouldn't leave the cafe until nine o'clock. He knew which room in the house she slept in, and he'd have to wait until he saw a lamplight in the room, then try to attract her attention.

He could only hope he wouldn't be taken for a prowler or a window peeper and get shot.

Next day, riding at a steady trot, he topped the pass before noon and looked down on the immense, sprawling upland valley of South Park. This late in the year the clumps of grass were straw-like, and hundreds of acres were covered with the blue-gray sagebrush. Small islands of pine and fir stuck up here and there, and the hills to the north and east were covered with green pine, patched with aspens. The aspens were mostly bare of leaves now.

At his horse's feet, glittering mica among the granite rocks caught the sunlight. Mica, also known as fool's gold, had excited and then disappointed many a greenhorn. Overhead, the sky was a canopy of blue. It was a beautiful scene, Tom acknowledged, and it was no wonder that an early explorer had looked down from the same pass and wrote in his diary that this would one day be an empire.

But, Shannon thought with a grim smile, whoever he was, he hadn't spent a winter in the South Park country. Good winter grazing land—most of the time. But Tom had heard of blizzards that decimated herds of cattle.

Down there far enough west to be out of sight was the town of Fortune. He rode on and came to his homestead about noon. He dismounted and walked around the burned-out ruins, trying to hold down the bitter bile in his throat. It was the second time in his life he had been burned out.

The war. Union troops went through his home country, setting fire to everything that would burn. The house, barn, sheds, crops, everything. They didn't have to do that. It was just plain meanness. They left his mother and sister a piece of land but nothing to farm it with. When the war ended and Tom came home, he was sick with bitterness. Everything was gone. He was so bitter he had to leave. Go west. For the next two years he had tried to forget and forgive. It wasn't easy, but he had managed to do that.

Now he was burned out again, and again it was just plain meanness.

He mounted and rode in a big circle around the ruins, hoping to see some of his cattle and horses. He saw no livestock at all. No doubt scattered far and wide. One of his horses was a buckskin gelding, eight years old, and an especially good horse. He was hoping he would find his horses and be able to ride up to that one and catch him. Instead, all he saw were two riders off to the south. Probably Running W riders.

If he hadn't been a fugitive he would have approached the two and asked if they had seen any of his stock. As it was, he turned his horse around and rode in a different direction, riding at a slow trot, trying not to look suspicious. When he looked back they were out of sight.

It was waiting time again. He loosened the cinch and allowed the horse to graze as he waited for dark. On second thought he tightened the cinch and mounted. He knew a place about a mile uphill from his burned-out cabin that was a good camping spot. He rode there and again dismounted and allowed the horse to graze.

There, grass, water, and firewood were plentiful, and the spot was ringed on three sides by hills. He gathered wood for a fire, but didn't light it. He only wanted to have it ready to light when he came back after dark. Now, he untied the tarp- covered roll from behind the saddle and ate a double handful of dried fruit. He realized he had been eating too little and had no doubt lost some weight, but he felt strong.

He grinned and said to himself, "One of these days I'm going to have to start living better." The grin vanished as he thought of Mary. When was he going to start living better? And what was he going to do about her?

Dark came somewhere around seven o'clock, he figured, and he'd have to wait another hour and a half. It would take about forty-five minutes to ride to Fortune and sneak around in back of Mary's house. He didn't want to get there too early. He ate more dried fruit, smoked, and waited. Finally, he tightened the cinch again and mounted. Whatever was going to happen that night was soon to happen.

Leaving his camp supplies behind, he rode down out of the hills onto the plains, riding at a trot in the dark. The horse, with its excellent night vision, had no trouble getting around the sagebrush and the rocks. He guessed it was about nine o'clock when he first saw the dim lights of Fortune. Instead of riding down the main street, he came into the town from the north, past the cemetery, past a handful of tar-paper shacks occupied by the unsuccessful gold prospectors. He rode at a walk now, and the clip-clop of the horse's hooves on the hard-packed street announced to the residents of the shacks that a rider was going past. No one looked out.

A short distance farther were the better houses, the wood-frame three- and four-room houses, built of lumber from the sawmill. Dim lights illuminated a few of the windows. Some of the houses had curtains in the windows, an indication that women lived in them. Others had bare glass, and some had blankets hung over the windows.

He turned down the alley behind Mary's house and wished his horse's hooves didn't make so much noise. The house, when he got behind it, was dark. Mary's late husband had built a board fence around the back half of the lot the house stood on, and Tom stopped his horse outside the fence and waited.

He wanted a smoke, but the burning end of a cigarette was too easy to see in the dark. He didn't want to be seen. Wait. Then he saw a light in the house, moving. Someone had come in the front door, lit a lamp, and was carrying it through the house. Tom had no way of knowing whether it was Mary or the woman who shared the house with her. Now another lamp was lit, and it was in Mary's bedroom.

Shannon tied his horse to a fence post, crawled over the fence, and approached the bedroom window. He had two problems: getting there and attracting Mary's attention without being seen and without scaring a scream out of her, and getting there before she started undressing for the night.

Moving swiftly but quietly, he approached the window. It was Mary brushing her brown hair. Tom rapped softly on the window. Mary started unbuttoning the top of her long dress. He rapped harder. She stopped what she was doing and listened. He rapped again. A startled look came over her face, and she glanced fearfully at the window. He rapped again and whispered, "Mary. It's Tom." She didn't hear his whisper and stood transfixed, as if trying to decide whether to run. He spoke louder, "Mary."

Then she heard him. She came to the window and peered out. "Mary," he said, "it's Tom."

"Tom?" She saw him, but wasn't sure she recognized him with his beard and the deputy's hat.

"It's me, Mary."

She recognized his voice, and her mouth opened in surprise. "Tom? Tom, wait right there. I'll be right out." She blew out the lamp and hurried to the back door.

"Over here, Mary."

She was in his arms, hugging and kissing him, crying softly and moaning, "Tom, Tom. My God, Tom."

He held her tight and buried his face in her hair, feeling the good woman feel of her and smelling the good woman smell. He wanted to wrap himself around her.

Finally, she leaned back and ran her fingers across his beard. "Tom, I almost died with worry. How are you? Are you injured? Are you hungry?"

"A little hungry, but all right. I...I had to come back, Mary."

She threw her arms around his neck again and hugged and kissed him some more. Her warm, soft body was pushed against him. When she leaned back the second time, she let her fingers wander over his face, his eyes, his lips. "Let's go in the house, Tom."

"Is the other woman around?"

"No. She left Fortune."

"You're living alone?"

"Yes. I'll fix you something to eat."

"Better go in ahead of me and shut all the window curtains. I'm a wanted man, you know."

"All right. Wait just a minute." She slipped from his arms and went inside. He saw her close the heavy curtains across her bedroom window and across the kitchen window. The entrance to the back door was dark when she whispered, "It's all right now."

He stepped inside and habitually removed his hat. She took him by the hand and led him to her bedroom where a coal-oil lamp put out a dim light. She gasped when she saw his face. "Oh, my. You look half-starved." She hugged and kissed him again. "Oh, my poor Tom. How have you survived? And"—her eyes went wide—"what is this?" She touched the bloodspot on the left side of his shirt.

"Had a little argument with a man and a gun. It's just a scratch, though."

"Let's see." She unbuttoned his shirt and pulled his shirttail out.

"Hey, wait a minute, now, you—"

"Hush. I know what a man looks like. I'm a widow, remember. You lie down there on that bed and let me put something on it."

He looked down at the wound himself. "It's better. It's healing."

"Lie down. I'll get something."

Sitting on the edge of the bed, he ran his hands over his hair and beard, fingered the sore spot on the side of his head, and wished he could make himself more presentable. She came from the kitchen with a bottle of rubbing alcohol.

"This will sting."

It stung, but he didn't let it show on his face. Mary found a clean handkerchief, put it over the wound, and wrapped a strip of cloth she tore from a worn-out petticoat around his stomach to hold it in place.

"Now. Tell me how that happened and everything."

"It's a long story, Mary. I walked to Tarryall, bought a horse, and rode back." He buttoned his shirt and tucked his shirttail in.

"Let's get some food in you, and some coffee, first."

"I've got a horse tied out back. I'd better bring him inside the fence."

"All right. I'll put the coffee on."

CHAPTER 15

He ate a meal of potato soup, homemade bread smothered in apple butter, and coffee. She apologized for not having more food in the house and explained that she took most of her meals at the cafe. "Tomorrow I'll cook something and feed you a real meal."

"Tomorrow..." He shrugged. He didn't know what to say about tomorrow.

But it was a subject that would have to be discussed. They both knew it. She waited until he finished his meal and rolled a cigarette.

"What...I'm almost afraid to ask, Tom, but what do you plan to do? Are you going to leave again? Do you want me to go with you?"

A grim smile turned up the corners of his mouth. "I reckon I'll have to leave. I can't be seen anywhere near here. Every man in the county has a license to shoot me on sight."

"Then, I'm going with you."

He shook his head sadly. "I can't ask you to do that. I'll always be a wanted man. You can't live that way, looking over your shoulder all the time."

"I'm going. If you want me."

"Lord knows I want you, Mary. But you'd be better off without me."

"Will you let me decide who I'm better off with or without?"

He looked down at his empty coffee cup. "It's a tough decision to make. I came back after I heard about what's going on around here, and I was worried about you. I don't think it's safe for you here." His

83

eyes were full of pain when he looked up at her. "I just don't know what to do."

They sat at the kitchen table and talked, and she could see the weariness in his face. "Let's get you to bed. You need rest."

"No, I'd better leave. I don't want to get you in trouble."

"You can stay until just before daylight."

"Mary, I have to decide what to do."

"We, Tom. We have to decide."

"Sure, uh..."

"All right, let's look at the whole thing rationally."

He had to smile at her way of talking, and he remembered that she was a reader.

"Someone shot Scott Wheeler. It wasn't you. The question is, Who? If we could find the answer to that question, you'd be able to live a normal life again."

He leaned forward, put his elbows on the table, and put his fists under his chin. "Wish I knew how to find out."

"I've been asking questions of everyone I know who comes in the cafe. It's strange. Scott Wheeler was a braggart and a bully. He was kicking an old man when you intervened, and he threatened you with a gun. Yet, I haven't been able to learn of another incident that could have made anyone mad enough at him to kill him."

"Most men just ignored him, but there is bound to be somebody who hated him."

"I've asked and asked. So far I have learned nothing."

A sigh came from his lips. "That's why it was so easy to convict me. I was the only one who tangled with him. And there was that percussion cap."

"Yes. That's another thing. You didn't leave it there, so someone else did. Someone else shot Scott Wheeler and left evidence that pointed to you. It was deliberate."

Nodding, he said, "I've thought of that too. But I can't for the life of me figure out who. Or why."

"Could it be someone at the Running W? I mean, you're grazing cattle on land that V.C. Wheeler considers his. And someone burned down your cabin. Could it be—No. I've tried to find a way to tie the Running W to what happened, and I can't. V.C. Wheeler wouldn't shoot his own son."

"No. And his foreman, Zack Parmell, was playing poker at the Salty Dog when young Wheeler was shot."

She touched his arm and looked into his face. "I'm not giving up. You were deliberately set up, and I'm going to keep on trying to find out who did it."

Shrugging, he said, "I'd sure like to find out. There's nothing I'd like better. But as long as I stay around here, I'll have to sneak around in the dark."

"You can eat and sleep here, but...you're right, you can't be seen."

He stood. "I've got a camp up north of my homestead. I'd better go on back. I'll sneak to town tomorrow night and we'll talk about what to do."

She stood with him. "You don't have to go yet."

"Yeah, if I stay any longer I'll be asleep and I might not wake up before daylight."

"I'll wake you up."

"No, I'll go. I'll be back."

She wrapped her arms around his neck and hugged him. Her kiss was so sweet he didn't want it to end. "I'm just so happy you came back, Tom. I don't know what's in store for us, but I'm so happy you came back."

His voice was husky. "Yeah, I had to come back. I had to see you again."

"We'll meet here tomorrow night?"

"Yeah, but don't leave the cafe early. Don't do or say anything unusual. We're taking a chance."

"Don't worry. I'm getting to be quite the evasive woman."

He blew out the lamp and went out the back door into the darkness. He found his horse, led it through the gate, and mounted. "Come on, old feller," he said quietly, "let's get back to our camp and get this saddle off your back."

A cold wind came up during the night, and Shannon's two blankets and the tarp weren't enough to keep him warm. He shivered in the cold and slept fitfully. At daylight he went to the creek and found it frozen along the edges. Winter was just ahead. He splashed cold water on his face, moved his horse from one grazing spot to another, built a fire, and fried bacon.

As soon as his bacon was done, he put out the fire and ate huddled under a tree with a blanket wrapped around his shoulders. The cold didn't bother the horse, but he said, "Better start growing some long winter hair, old feller. Ben Stumps kept you in a barn too much, and nature didn't know it was time to get ready for winter."

He stood and walked around stamping his feet. A fire would have kept him warm, but he didn't want to take a chance on someone seeing the smoke. The wind cleaned off the rest of the aspen leaves and scattered brown pine needles over the ground. He wondered if his cattle had found some winter grazing country yet. They would drift until they did, but how far would they drift? And his horses. Would he ever see them again?

Well, he thought, right now I've got more important things to worry about. Like who killed Scott Wheeler. Mary had been asking questions, but had learned nothing. Who could he question that Mary hadn't already questioned? Had to be someone. And what would he ask? Well, for a start, who left that cap from his rifle near Wheeler's body? Whoever he was, he had to have gotten it from Shannon's cabin. Someone, when Tom wasn't there, had come by, seen the cap on the ground, picked it up, and carried it away. Had the person planned on killing someone and making it look as though Tom had done it?

Tom mulled it over in his mind. Why?

All right, let's see now. A gang has been terrorizing this part of the country. That means the gang members live in this part of the country. Where? Have they got a hideout? Maybe that's it. Scott Wheeler was always riding. Sometimes with a crew of cowboys and sometimes by himself. Did he see something the gang didn't want him to see? If he did, why didn't he report it to the deputy marshal?

Maybe, just maybe, he saw something the gang didn't want him to see and he didn't realize it. Maybe he didn't know that what he saw would worry the gang. Did he find their camp? No, he would have told the deputy. Did he see one of the gang members? Doubtful. He'd have told the deputy.

No one knew who the gang members were, anyway. They always kept their faces covered when they were robbing and killing, and when they went into town they changed clothes, horses, and everything.

Another question: Why didn't they bother the merchants in Fortune? That when Shannon thought about it, wasn't hard to figure out. They needed supplies from the merchants. They didn't want to drive the merchants out of business.

So the gang did go into Fortune and they had managed to keep their identities a secret. Who were they? Fortune was a mining and lumber town, and also a cattle town. Working men came and went. Strangers were seen every day. That former rebel Tom had tangled with, the one with the pillbox cap, he no doubt shoved that cap inside his shirt and wore something else when he went to town.

That meant they lived in this part of the country. They had a change of clothes and they had more than one horse apiece. They had a hideout. Someone, sometime, would come across it. Ugh, Tom grunted when he thought about it. Maybe someone already had, and hadn't lived to tell about it.

Not Scott Wheeler, though. He would have told.

At noon, Tom Shannon ate a cold lunch of dried apricots and the bread and apple butter that Mary had given him. Tonight, he promised himself, he was going to eat a real meal with his feet under a table. Tonight he and Mary would talk it over and try again to figure out who might have killed Scott Wheeler. Between the two of them, they might figure it out.

CHAPTER 16

Having nothing else to do, Tom Shannon wrapped his two blankets around himself and dozed under a ponderosa. The wind sighed and moaned and sometimes whistled shrilly through the trees. The horse, after eating its fill of the tall brown grass, lay down too, but stayed right side up, with its legs under its body. At dusk, Shannon led the horse to the creek and let it drink, then saddled it. He ate some more dried apricots and waited. About an hour and a half after dark, he mounted and rode downhill.

He rode into town and down the same alley behind Mary's house. He dismounted and led the horse through the wooden gate in her backyard, tied it to a fence post. The back side of the house was dark, and Tom wasn't sure Mary was at home. He approached the back door quietly and tapped lightly. Immediately, she opened the door and whispered, "Tom?" Inside, she was wrapped in his arms again, and their lips met and stayed together for several long moments. Then she said, "I've been waiting in the dark, I think it's all right to light a lamp now."

"The dark." He grinned. "Seems like I've been living in the dark a lot lately. I ought to have eyes like an owl."

"Sit down and I'll feed you. I had to eat at the cafe. If I hadn't, someone might have wondered why."

The meal was delicious: roast beef, brown gravy, mashed potatoes, good homemade bread, coffee. He ate until his stomach could hold no more, then leaned back in his chair and rolled a smoke.

"That makes the world worth living in," he said. "When a man can eat like that, he can survive anything."

"Well"—she smiled and sat on his lap—"there are other worthwhile things too, you know."

"Oh?" He grinned with her. "Like what?"

"Well, there's, uh..."

"A good woman," he answered for her. "A man needs a good woman." He pulled her to him. "You're a good woman, Mary."

"Would you like to spend the night, Tom? You'll be safe here until daylight."

"Looking like this? I probably don't smell too good either."

"You could take a bath. I've got a bathtub and I can heat some water."

He studied her face in the lamplight. "You mean it, don't you?"

"Yes. I'm shameless, aren't I?"

Pulling her close again, he murmured in her hair, "You're a good woman. But"—he sat back in his chair—"we've got things to talk about."

"Oh. Yes, we do, don't we." She stood and ran her hands down the front of her long dress, smoothing it out. "More coffee?"

"Please, ma'am."

She poured another cup and sat in a chair across the table. "Any ideas?"

"No ideas. A lot of questions but no answers."

"Like what?"

"All right, let's start with this: Scott Wheeler did a lot of riding in the mountains, keeping an eye on Running W cattle and looking for cattle that needed doctoring, and all those things that cowboys do. Now, we've already figured someone deliberately framed me for Scott Wheeler's murder, and that someone just happened to have a used-up cap from my rifle. Only, he didn't just happen to have it. He had to have picked it up at my cabin before that night. He had to have been planning to kill Scott Wheeler and make it look like I did it."

Shannon paused to take a sip of coffee. "I've asked myself why, and I don't know why. Could it be that young Wheeler saw something that someone didn't want him to see? If so, what? And why didn't he report it to Deputy Atwell?"

"Hmmm." She put her elbows on the table and her chin in her hands. "He saw something or somebody." She frowned. "And whatever or whoever it was, he didn't think it was important. But...whoever it was wished he hadn't been seen, and was afraid that Scott Wheeler might eventually connect that incident with something else, and—"

Tom finished the thought. "He figured Wheeler might, sooner or later, put two and two together."

"And he decided that Scott Wheeler had to die, and he hoped he could blame it on you. That's why he went to your cabin when you weren't there and picked up one of your rifle caps."

"Yeah, and he got lucky when Wheeler and I had an argument in the Salty Dog that night. He might have been planning to shoot Wheeler out in the hills someplace and hope folks would think the two of us met, argued over grazing land, and shot it out."

"That makes sense, Tom."

"Yeah, but that brings us back to question number one: Who?"

"Hmmm." She got up and pumped a pot of water from the short-handled kitchen pump. She put the water on the two-lid stove, then fed more wood to the stove. Tom rolled another smoke and realized he was smoking too much.

"It was someone in the Salty Dog," she said, sitting again. "He saw and heard what happened between you and Wheeler and saw his chance."

"Yeah. Had to be."

"Were there many men in there that night?"

"Quite a few. I can't remember who. There was Zack Parmell. He and young Wheeler came in while V.C. Wheeler and I were standing at the bar talking business. Mr. Wheeler wanted to buy one of my bulls. I didn't see them come in." Tom took a drag on his cigarette. "Come to think of it, why didn't father and son speak to one another when young Wheeler came in? That's strange. Old V.C. acted like he didn't even see him."

"Are you sure he did see him?"

"Maybe he didn't, but young Wheeler saw his dad."

"Hmmm. That is strange."

"Yeah, and young Wheeler was in a bad mood. A real bad

mood. He tried to pick a fight with me, but I didn't want to fight."

"He did? How did he do that?"

"Oh, he started hoorawing me about you."

"Oh?" Her eyebrows went up. "What did he say?"

"Nothing much. It didn't mean anything."

"What, Tom?"

He didn't want to tell her, but he saw that determined look on her face and knew she'd get it out of him one way or another. "He said a lumberjack was courting you."

"He did? Who? Oh, I'll bet he saw me talking to Orville."

"Orville?"

"He's an off-bearer at the sawmill. He's a bachelor and he eats at the Silver Lode. He likes to talk, but he's a gentleman."

"Uh-huh."

She got up, hurried around the table, and sat on his lap again. Her eyes had gone from serious to mischievous. "What do you mean, 'uh-huh'? Do you want me to pull your beard?"

In spite of himself he had to laugh. Suddenly, all his worries were gone and he had one of the most desirable women in the world sitting on his lap, teasing him. For the first time since the night he was arrested, he felt like laughing. "You do that and I'll spank you."

"Oh yeah?" She gave his beard a tug. He scooted his chair back, picked her up, and turned her over his knees. She squealed and giggled. Holding her down with one hand he smacked her across the bottom with the other. Her bottom was... Lord. Suddenly, he let go his hold on her and let her up. This had to stop. This was not the time.

She sat up and saw the stern look on his face. "This is not the time for it, is that what you're thinking?"

"Yeah." He grinned sheepishly.

She considered that, then said, "I'm going to heat some water and give you a bath, and then we'll see."

"But..."

"I'd shave off your beard, but it makes you a little harder to recognize."

"But..."

She pumped another large pot of water, put it on the stove, and fed the fire. "Now, let's get your shirt off and see about that wound."

"But..."

The last thing she said to him that night was, "Don't worry, darling, I'll wake you up before daylight."

CHAPTER 17

He was back at his camp just after dawn where he off-saddled his horse and tied it out to graze. He cooked his bacon over a small fire, and ate it with the biscuits Mary had given him. Rested now, he couldn't sit still.

If he had another horse, he decided, he could spend the day riding east in the high country, the direction he'd been traveling when he was confronted by two outlaws. With luck and a little tracking skill, he might, just might, come across the outlaw hideout. But his one horse had spent the night tied to a fence post with a saddle on its back. It would be foolish to ride his one horse down. He had to keep that one fresh.

Lord, he wished he could find and catch his good buckskin gelding. And that reminded him too of the horse he'd ridden to town the morning he was arrested. What had the deputy done with it, and his saddle, his good saddle?

Dawn came with the sky clear but the temperature below freezing. The creek was frozen along the edges again, and the yellow aspen leaves were swirling on the ground. Across the creek, the cinquefoil was brown, yellow, and red, and the leaves of the wild geraniums and wild rosebushes were bright red. Tom could see every color imaginable from where he was sitting. Soon, he knew, everything would be covered with snow.

Feeling more restless with each passing minute, he walked around, swinging his arms to keep warm. He picked up his rifle and crossed the creek at a narrow spot and prowled through the cinquefoil on the other side. Glancing back at his camp, he knew it would be easy to spot if anyone happened along, but there was nothing he could do about it. He couldn't hide a grazing horse.

He walked up the creek, angling toward a stand of pine and spruce uphill from there. He came to an old beaver pond with about fifty square feet of black mud on the downstream side of it. Standing quietly and watching, he saw no beaver, and guessed the beaver had been trapped a couple of years earlier.

What he did see were elk tracks, cows and calves, and off to one side the larger tracks of a bull elk. It was rutting season for the bulls, he knew, a time when they gathered harems of cows and challenged other bulls for the territory.

With nothing else to do, and too restless to go back to his camp and just sit, Shannon walked on into the timber. When he was out of sight of his camp he stopped, sat on a small boulder, and smoked a cigarette. A weird high whistle broke the quiet, and he listened and finally recognized it. It was a nerve-tingling, high-note bugling; a bull elk, issuing his challenge to any other of his sex and species that might be within hearing distance. Tom had heard of hunters who had learned to imitate that call and bring bull elk within easy shooting range. For want of nothing better to do, he wet his lips and tried it. On the third try, he got out a four-note whistle, then grinned to himself. A bull would have to be pretty dumb to be fooled by that.

But a few minutes later he heard the sound of tree limbs cracking, and the *thunk, thunk, whack* of a large animal moving in the timber and making no effort to be quiet. He whistled again and got an answer. Something like an army bugler gone crazy.

Just to see what would happen, Shannon sat still on his boulder and waited. After a few more minutes, the snapping of branches was closer, and finally he could see the bull, standing under a tall spruce, head up. A beautiful animal, with its heavy brown neck fur, tan body, and a wide set of antlers. It hadn't seen him, but it had sensed something unusual. An easy target, and Tom had his rifle, but he didn't want to shoot anything. For a long moment, the bull stood there, and then decided that whatever had issued the challenge was something it didn't understand and wanted no part of. It wheeled and ran off, back the way it had come.

Tom had to grin. "Maybe you aren't so dumb after all," he said quietly.

He smoked another cigarette, vowed to quit smoking so much when he got his life back to normal, then snorted. "Huh. When I get my life back to normal. Sure." He got up and walked again, downhill, back toward his camp. Before he left the cover of the timber he stopped and took a long look. His horse was still grazing. Everything was the way he'd left it. Looked safe. He walked on, then stopped suddenly. The horse had its head up now, nostrils flared, nickering.

That told Tom that another horse was near.

Immediately he dropped to the ground, stayed there for a long moment, then got to his knees so he could see over the cinquefoil. Nothing at his camp moved except the horse. Its head was still up, and it was looking toward a timbered hill on the west side of his camp. Someone was there. Someone on a horse.

Squatting, Shannon tried to figure out what to do. How many were over there? Probably only one man. More than one would be easy to see. Well, maybe not easy, but possible. Whoever he was, he was waiting over there, curious to find out whose camp that was, but afraid to approach until he did find out. A man could get killed riding up to a stranger's camp.

Tom considered staying put, trying to outwait the man. If he waited long enough the other man's curiosity would get the better of him and he'd ride up. Or give up and ride on, believing it best to mind his own business. Tom waited, staying low. Nothing moved except the horse. More waiting. It seemed to him that the two things he'd done most since breaking out of jail were waiting and stumbling around in the dark. Damn, he was getting tired of that.

The cinquefoil grew thicker upstream, and if he could get up there without being seen, he could cross the creek in the timber and maybe stay out of sight and get around behind the man. Then what? Shoot him?

No, he thought, just see who he is and then decide what to do. But no, he wasn't going to shoot anyone if he could help it. All right, crawl.

On his hands and knees again, he crawled, hanging on to the

rifle. This was something else he had done before, and he was getting damned tired of this too. Crawl and quit your bellyaching, he told himself. Stopping now and then to take another look at his camp, he crawled on until he got into the timber. There, he took another long look back at his camp. Everything was the same, but his horse still had its head up, looking to the west. The man, or men, were still there. He crawled farther until he was out of sight of his camp and the man or men on the hill, then stood up and waded across the creek, getting his feet wet, but not caring. He walked carefully but swiftly until he was on the other side of the hill west of his camp, then stopped and listened again.

No sound. Not a living creature in sight. Maybe the man had left. Maybe not. Keeping low but staying on his feet, Shannon hurried from one tree to another. At each tree he stopped and listened. Quiet. He moved to a spot he believed was just west of the top of the hill the man was on, just over the hill from the man. Still no sound. He waited, ears straining. Should hear a horse's feet moving, something. Nothing.

His rifle in his hands, he crept to the top of the hill. He saw the horse.

Another long pause, watching, listening. Only one horse. One horse meant one man. Where was the man? The horse, a gray, was tied to a tree limb by the bridle reins. Tom crept closer.

He saw the brand on the horse's left hip. A Running W. He saw the man.

The man was lying on his stomach behind a bunch of small boulders, watching Tom's camp below. At first Tom didn't recognize him, then after a good look he did. Zack Parmell, foreman of the Running W.

Tom crept closer. He held his rifle aimed, ready, the hammer back. He said softly, "Zack."

CHAPTER 18

A coiled rattlesnake couldn't have moved faster. The ranch foreman flopped over onto his back and reached for the six-gun on his right hip at the same instant.

"Hold it." Shannon had the rifle leveled, Parmell's chest in the sights.

The cowboy's hand was on his gun butt. "I'll shoot, Zack."

The hand stopped.

"Don't move. Move and I'll put a bullet in you." Tom approached, slowly, carefully, keeping the cowboy's chest in his gunsights. When he was close enough, he bent his knees, eyes on Parmell's face, squatted, and lifted the pistol from the holster. Then he stepped back.

"Just stay right there. One move and I'll shoot." Tom grinned a dry, mirthless grin. "I'm a killer, you know."

"I had a hunch it was you," Parmell said.

"Now you know. What're you going to do about it?"

"Kill you if I get a chance."

"Then, I'll have to see you don't get a chance."

"You'll have to kill me."

"If it comes down to you or me, it'll be you."

Shannon backed off a few more steps and squatted on his heels. He put the rifle on the ground at his feet, but kept Parmell's pistol cocked and ready. For a time, neither man spoke, just glared at one another.

"Looking for cattle that haven't drifted down yet, Zack?"

"What do you care?"

"Do you really think I killed Scott Wheeler?"

"Hell, yes. You were tried according to law."

"You were on the jury. The others walked across the room without any doubt on their minds, but you waited a couple of seconds. Why did you wait?"

"I was deliberating, like the judge said to do."

"You were deliberating alone. You must have had some doubt. The judge mentioned a reasonable doubt, too."

"I had a little doubt, but not what I'd call a reasonable one."

Tom mulled that over. "Why did you have a doubt?"

"I didn't. Not after deliberating."

"There must have been something about the whole thing that didn't sit right with you."

"Wasn't nothing."

"Did Scott Wheeler have any enemies?"

"None. None that would've shot him in the back."

"You can't be sure about that, can you?"

"Reasonable sure."

"He was a braggart and he liked to show off. He had to have made someone mad at him."

Parmell said nothing to that.

"All right, tell me this. Why didn't he speak to V.C. Wheeler when he came into the Salty Dog that night?"

"That's none of your business."

"The hell it isn't. I'm accused of killing him. Every damn thing about him is my business."

Parmell was quiet.

"You afraid of something, Zack? Are you afraid I might find out who really killed Scott Wheeler? Did you have something to do with it?"

"Me? Why me?"

"Oh, I don't know. Maybe he wanted you fired. Did you have an argument with Scott Wheeler?" The ranch foreman's eyes flicked between Tom's face and the gun in his hand. Shannon sat back on the seat of his pants, his feet in front of him, and held his gun arm on his right knee. He kept the gun pointed at Parmell's chest.

"It wasn't me," the cowboy said. "I was in the Salty Dog when the shooting happened. Everybody knows that."

"Yeah. So it wasn't you. You could have hired someone to do it."

"That's a goddamn lie."

"So, answer my question: Why didn't father and son speak to each other?"

"That's none of your—"

Tom cut him off. "Don't give me that bull. I'm a desperate man, Zack. I came within a hair of being hung for a killing I didn't do, my cabin and shed were burned down, my horses were run off, and my cattle are drifting all over the country. Who burned my cabin down?"

"I don't know."

"You know something. If you didn't, you'd answer my question."

The ranch foreman's mouth opened, shut, opened again. "Old V.C. and his kid had an argument that day."

"What kind of an argument?"

"The usual kind. They were always yelling at each other."

"Yeah? What did they argue about?"

"Hell, I don't know. Anything and everything."

"I take it, then, that they didn't get along so good."

"Didn't get along at all."

"They yelled at one another, huh?"

"Wasn't nothing unusual. They argued all the time."

"Must have been pretty mad at one another that night."

"Sure. But they never stayed mad. Sometimes they didn't speak to each other for a day or two, but they always made up."

"Why didn't they get along?"

"Hell, you know, old V.C. was a colonel in the Union army and he'd had his fill of guns and fighting, and his kid couldn't get enough of it. He was always practicing with that Colt six-shooter of his."

"V.C. was a colonel?"

"Yeah. He didn't go around telling everybody about it. He told me once, and said the war was over and he wanted it to stay over."

"Did he have any grudges against the rebels?"

"No. I know he didn't 'cause I was a reb myself."

"You were? Did you keep your weapon when the war was over?"

"Naw. I picked up one of those Henry repeaters on the battlefield one day, you know, one of those Yankee rifles, and I done just like you, I lit out. Came west. Got a job riding for the Running W and got promoted to foreman."

"Quick promotion. There must have been other men around here who knew more about cattle and the open range than you."

"There was. But I was an officer in the Army and I knew how to run a crew, and..." Parmell paused.

"What?"

"I think the colonel—V.C.—wanted to make up for what happened in the war."

"Uh-huh. Hmmm."

They were quiet a moment, but Parmell didn't take his eyes off the gun and Tom didn't relax his grip on it.

"Tell me something else, Zack. You stayed at the Salty Dog after I left. Did anything happen?"

"Nothing."

"No brawls, arguments, or anything?"

"Nothing."

"What did Scott Wheeler do?"

"He drank and played faro. Or maybe it was blackjack."

"Were there many men playing faro?"

"Only a few. Most of us in the gambling mood got up a poker game."

"Did Scott have an argument with the faro dealer?"

"No. They played peaceful."

"Did he win or lose?"

"Don't know. Not much either way, I hear."

"Hmmm." For a second, Tom let his gaze drop to the ground, his mind working. Out of the corner of his eyes he caught a movement, and he looked up and tightened his grip on the gun. "Don't move, damn it."

"You wouldn't shoot me if I rolled a smoke, would you?"

"Go ahead, but move slow. Make a sudden move and this gun

will go off."

Tom could have used a smoke himself as he watched Zack Parmell roll one and light it. But he didn't dare put the gun down, and he'd never learned to roll a cigarette with one hand.

He said, "Are you sure nothing happened while Scott Wheeler played faro?"

"Nothing. Like I told you."

"Nothing at all?"

"Only thing that happened was a gent I never saw before came in and said something to the dealer. I didn't hear what he said."

"Could Wheeler have heard?"

"Don't know. They whispered."

"Did the man leave then?"

"Naw. He stood at the bar and had a drink of whiskey. I think he left after that."

"How soon after that did Wheeler leave?"

"Not real soon. He quit playing and had a drink at the bar himself."

"Uh-huh. Hmmm. Then he left?"

"Yeah."

"Who left first, Wheeler or the man who whispered to the dealer?"

"Why, I don't know. Wasn't watching that close. Why?"

Tom shrugged. "I guess it doesn't matter. What's the faro dealer's name?"

"Barrett, I think. Yeah, it's Henry Barrett."

"He been dealing faro there very long?"

"A few months."

"Know anything at all about him?"

"Naw."

"Ever hear anything about him?"

"Naw. He minds his own business as far as I know."

"If I remember right, he carries a gun."

"Sure. Most men do around here."

"It's a pearl handled revolver, isn't it? And if I remember right, he carries it low, the way Scott Wheeler carried his."

"Yeah, that's right. I wouldn't want to try to outdraw him."

"Hmmm."

Parmell smoked his cigarette. Tom studied his face. He believed the ranch foreman was telling the truth. For some reason, he was talking freely. Why? The horse at Tom's camp nickered again, but Parmell's horse, tied to a tree, didn't nicker back.

"You're answering my questions, Zack. How come?"

Parmell inhaled deeply and blew the smoke out slowly. "They seem like fair questions."

"If I remember right, the stage was robbed the day after I was arrested. Or was it a couple of days later?"

"It was two days later."

"And Deputy Atwell was killed a couple of days after I ran."

"Yeah."

"How was he killed?"

"Shot from ambush. Same way you killed Scott Wheeler."

A wry grin touched Shannon's lips. "You think I killed both of them?"

Parmell only stared at him.

"Was the deputy shot down in the street?"

"No. He was trying to track you down."

"Oh." That, Shannon thought, sure made it look bad for him. "Does anyone think I did it?"

"No. Old Orville over at the sawmill was riding with Atwell, trying to help, and he got a glimpse of the shooter. He didn't look like you."

"What did he look like?"

"Wore a cap with a bill on it. Riding a bay horse."

Tom thought it over, then said, "I think I'd know the shooter if I saw him again. Sounds like the jackleg I met up there." He nodded to the higher hills.

"You did?"

"Yeah. Left one man dead."

"How?"

With a shrug of his shoulders, Tom said, "It's a long story. Right now I'm trying to save my own hide."

"Yeah, and how're you going to do that?"

"That's a problem." Shannon was worried now about what to

do with Zack Parmell. Let him go, and he'd round up some men and come looking for him. Kill him, and he really would be a murderer.

"Tell me something, Zack. What would you do if I let you get on your horse and get the hell away from here?"

"What would you expect me to do? Come back and try to find you."

"If you were holding this gun instead of me, my life wouldn't be worth a nickel, would it?"

"Nope."

"All right, I'll tell you what I'm going to do. I'm going to take your horse and gun and go down there and saddle my own horse and roll up my camp and leave. I'll tie your horse to something about a mile upstream. Just follow the creek and you'll find your horse and gun. But don't move till I break camp and get on my way."

CHAPTER 19

He rode Parmell's horse down the hill, caught and saddled his own horse, rolled up his camp, and rode upstream. About a mile on, he tied Parmell's horse to a tree and then headed west.

Keeping to a westerly course, he rode down onto the flats, around the town of Fortune, and took to the high hills again. There, he looked for and finally found another camping spot where the water and grass were plentiful. On the way he spotted a small bunch of cattle and out of curiosity rode closer to look them over. Two of the cows were his and the rest wore the Running W brand. He hoped to see his horses, but didn't.

With his one horse staked out again and grazing, he ate a double handful of dried apricots and a can of beans, and pondered his next move. His problems were mounting. Zack Parmell would tell everybody the wanted man was camping in the nearby hills, and they would be looking for him. Worse, they all knew he was courting the Widow Cress, and they would be watching her house.

Now he would have to stay away from Mary.

But dammit, he couldn't stay away from Mary. He had to see her. Hell, if he couldn't see Mary he might as well get on that horse and hightail it out of the country. There was no use staying anywhere near Fortune. There had to be a way to see her.

Well, he decided, there was only one way. He had to sneak into town in the dark again, and try to get Mary's attention while she was walking home from the Silver Lode Cafe. It was a three-block walk, and on her way she passed two alleys.

At dusk he saddled up again. Timing was important, and it wasn't going to be easy. He rode at a walk until dark, then came into town from the west, still staying away from the main street. He rode down a side street, down an alley, and dismounted in an alley that opened onto the main street.

He had no way of knowing what time it was, but he could see the Silver Lode from there and he could see it was still open for business. Just as the man who killed Scott Wheeler had, he was waiting in a dark alley for a certain person to come along. Skulking in the alley like a thief in the night. Standing back in the shadows, he could only hope that no one saw him, became suspicious, and demanded to know what he was doing there. Several times, men walked past the alley, but they didn't stop. A quarter moon cast some light, but not enough to recognize a man at any distance at all.

Come on, Mary.

A cigarette would have tasted good. No, can't strike a match. Too easy to see.

It seemed like an hour passed before the lights in the Silver Lode went out. Won't be long now, he thought.

He saw her. Dammit. A man was with her. The man was walking with her. A big man. Must have been six foot three. Bigger than that son of a bitch Ben Stumps at Tarryall. Was he going to walk her home? See that she got home safe?

Shannon groaned under his breath. Oh no. They were on his side of the street, heading for Mary's house. At her house they would have to part. She was expecting him. They stopped on the street. They stood there for a long moment. He could barely make them out in the dark. Their voices reached his ears, but he couldn't hear what they were saying.

The man left her, crossed the street, and turned down a side street. He was not only tall, he was broad. Mary came on, walking rapidly, her heels making tap-tapping sounds on the plank sidewalk. He stepped out of the shadows to where she could see him, and when she started past the alley he whispered, "Mary."

Again louder, "Mary."

She stopped.

"In here."

She glanced up and down the street and stepped into the alley, into his arms. Eventually, she stepped back. "I've got a message for you, darling."

"A message? From who?"

"Shhh. Let's go home and talk there."

"That's dangerous. They know I'm here and they know I'll be at your house. They'll be looking for me there."

"No they won't. That's one of the things I want to talk about."

"Sure, they know. I was seen."

"The message I have for you is from Zack Parmell. He said he won't tell. Not yet, anyway."

"He did? He said that?"

"Yes. So only he knows you've come back, and he isn't telling."

A heavy sigh of relief came from him. "Boy, I thought I was going to have to make love to you in this alley."

"Come on, let's go home. It's more comfortable there."

He walked, leading the horse with one hand, his other arm around her waist. At the front of her house, she whispered, "I'll go in and close all the blinds and open the back door."

"All right, I'll go around back and put my horse inside the fence again."

Mounted, he rode to the end of the block and turned down the alley. In the darkness, he could barely see the gate in the yard back of Mary's house, but he found it, led his horse through, and tied the animal to a fence post. I owe a lot to Mary's deceased husband for building this fence, he told himself. May he rest in peace.

With quiet steps he made his way to the back door, groped for the door handle, found it. The door was unlocked. He cracked it open. It was dark inside.

He stepped over the threshold and heard a muffled scream.

Someone grabbed him in a bear hug from behind. Someone strong. Something hit him on the head, knocking his hat off. Something hit him on the head again. A sharp pain flashed through his head. Another blow and another sharp flash of pain. He tried to free himself, to free his arms. He bucked, pitched, and stomped on someone's toes. The bear hug loosened a little. He kicked back and stomped on the toes again. Another muffled scream. Mary.

He bent forward, trying to throw the man behind him over his shoulder. Something hit him on the left ear, then on the head. He felt his knees buckle, and he knew he was going down. Another blow on the head and he was down on the floor, only barely conscious. The last thing he heard was Mary's scream.

CHAPTER 20

The light was dim. So dim he wasn't sure he was seeing a light. He lay still, trying to figure out where he was. He was lying on something cool. Cool and slick. Like a linoleum floor. He groaned.

"Hey," someone said, "he ain't dead after all. You didn't hit 'im hard enough, Sam'l."

"Let's get 'im up."

Two pairs of hands grabbed him by the arms and hair and lifted him up. His head was pounding so badly he couldn't think. He was only barely aware of what was happening. The hands sat him in a chair and someone behind him got hold of his hair and pulled his head back. He felt a sharp sting on the side of his neck.

"This here's a gen-u-ine bowie knife," a man's voice said. "One leetle move out of you and it'll slice your throat open like a busted watermelon."

Muffled grunts, groans, and screams came from somewhere in front of him. He tried to focus his eyes, but his head was held back so far he couldn't see anything.

Blood was trickling down his face, into his mouth. His blood. His head felt like it was full of wet sawdust, and each beat of his heart sent another sharp pain to his temples.

"Me first," another male voice said. "Ah got 'er gagged so she cain't holler."

"What'll I do with this'n?"

"Shit, ah don't care. Slit his goddamn throat. Me and this little

108

lady's got some business in the bedroom."

He recognized the voice, and wished now he'd killed the man when he had a chance.

"Leave some for me."

"Shit, it don't wear out."

"We ought to cut the cards or somethin' to see who goes first."

"Ain't got no cards."

His eyes were beginning to focus now, but the throbbing in his head made thinking difficult. He strained his eyes, trying to look down, trying to see Mary. A vague shape began to take form. Mary was sitting in a chair across the kitchen table. Her hands were behind the chair and a rag was tied around her head, across her mouth. Her eyes were wide with horror.

A man was behind her, untying her hands. "Well, shit, let's flip a coin. I got a four-bit piece."

Shannon flexed his fingers. They worked. He blinked, trying to clear his head. The pain wouldn't let up. Think, he told himself. What's happening?

Mary was standing now, swaying drunkenly. The man was still behind her, pawing her. She tried weakly to struggle out of his grasp. He chuckled cruelly.

"Don't be disagreeable, little lady, or old Job there'll cut your lover boy's throat."

She tried to scream, but all that came out was a muffled grunt.

The man moved around in front of her and hugged her, running his hands down the back of her long dress, over her hips. His voice was husky now. "You don't know how long it's been since I had a woman."

"Yeah," said the one behind Tom. "A feller'd think she wanted it, the way she shut all the winders so nobody could see the light."

"She was awaitin' for lover boy there," said the other one.

"Well, she ain't gonna be disappointed."

"Come on." She was being pulled by one arm toward the bedroom.

"Justa goddamn minute. We gotta flip a coin or somethin'."

The knife was against his throat. One little twist of the wrist and he'd die, strangling on his own blood. Think. He was sitting in a chair in the kitchen. A man he couldn't see had hold of his hair and was pulling his head back. The knife was in the man's left hand. Tom's hands were free. Could he get one arm up between the man's knife arm and his throat? Not likely.

"God damn it, what's the matter with you. It was my idee. I'm first."

"Like hell it was. I'm the one remembered this purty widder livin' in this big house all by herself."

"Shit, if it wasn't for me we wouldn't a knowed she had a man with 'er. You'd a waited here in the dark and he'd a shot you so full of holes you'd leak like a rusty bucket."

"Naw, he wouldn't. I'd of seen 'im too. You just happened to be the one lookin' out the winder and seen 'im first."

Had the pressure of the knife lessened? Could he move fast enough?

"Whatta you care? You never had a purty woman anyways. Shit, if it wasn't for the whores you'd be a virgin."

"Well, by God, we're gonna do this fair."

"Fair?" The man named Sam'l laughed a cruel laugh. "Tell you what. Go ahead and slit that sombitch's throat and we'll flip a coin."

Mary jumped, grunted, kicked, and tried to pull away.

"Not yet. Shit, long's we got a knife to his throat, she'll do anything we ast 'er to. Won't you, honey?"

"Yeah, that's right. You don't want to see lover boy's blood all over your kitchen floor, do you?" She shook her head violently.

"So come on now. Be nice. We ain't gonna hurt you. You've done it before."

She stood still, staring with terrified eyes at Tom.

Could he do it? He'd have to move as fast as he'd ever moved in his life. Which hand would be better? The right hand. That way maybe he could get his left arm around the man's head, wrestle him down. Tom flexed his fingers and blinked his eyes, trying to ready himself.

"Look how gentle she is now. Goddamn, I cain't wait. Get that goddamn half-dollar out and let's get this settled."

"Ain't you got a coin?"

"Let's see." Sam'l dug into his pants pocket and pulled out a gold eagle. "This'll do."

"Flip it on top of the table where I can see."

"All right. Here it goes. Heads I'm first." He flipped the heavy coin with his thumb and it landed with a *clank* on the table. "Goddamn, heads."

"You sure? Let's see."

The knife was no longer touching him. Now. Do it now.

Tom Shannon jerked his right hand up and across his chest, got hold of the hoodlum's wrist, pushed out with it.

"Hey, what—?"

He stood, got his knees straight, his right hand still hanging on to the man's left wrist. Now he got his left arm around the man's head and swung him around. They were facing one another, grunting, straining. Sam'l was coming, grabbing at the gun on his right hip. Tom got his left foot behind the hoodlum's left foot and shoved him backward. The hoodlum stumbled over Tom's foot and fell against the charging Sam'l. Both men went down, almost colliding with Mary. Tom let go of the first man and jumped on Sam'l, trying to wrestle the gun out of his hand. Sam'l was hanging on.

The man named Job rolled over and got up. He grabbed at Tom's hair again and tried to pull him off Sam'l. Tom refused to let go of the gun. He got his knees on Sam'l's stomach and bounced up and down. A loud grunt came from Sam'l, but still he hung onto the gun. Job gave up trying to pull Tom off his partner and grabbed for his own gun.

"Shoot 'im," Sam'l yelled. "Shoot the sombitch."

"Shit, it'll bring ever'body runnin'."

"Shoot 'im, goddamn it."

Tom's knees were on Sam'l's chest now, then his throat, then his face. Sam'l's grip on the gun relaxed. A gurgling came out of his throat. A gun barrel hit Tom a glancing blow on the top of his head, and another bright flash of pain shot through his brain. He rolled over onto his back, turning Sam'l's gun around.

Stopped.

He was looking up the bore of a gun in Job's hand. Job was grinning.

"So it'll bring somebody runnin'. It'll be worth it. You've

breathed your last breath, cowboy."

But he didn't shoot. Instead he was suddenly trying to fight off a wildcat. Mary was all over him, clawing, kicking, shoving. Tom heaved to his feet, got his left hand on Job's gun, and whipped him across the face with Sam'l's gun. Job went limp. Tom twisted the gun out of his hand.

Mary was grunting and groaning inside the gag in her mouth. Shannon stuck the gun inside his belt and quickly untied the gag. The first thing she said was, "Behind you, Tom." He swiveled in time to see Sam'l getting to his feet.

"Hold it." He had the gun in his hand again, leveled.

Sam'l knew he meant it, and stopped in a half squatting position.

For several seconds no one moved. Mary stood transfixed, eyes staring at Tom. Job was on his knees, groaning. Sam'l was sitting on his heels, looking at his own gun in Tom's hand. Shannon wanted to look at Mary, put his arms around her, but he didn't dare take his eyes off the two hoodlums.

Mary spoke first, her voice high, scared. "Get. Both of you. Get out of here."

"You want to let them go?" Tom spoke without moving his eyes.

"Yes."

She was right. What else could he do? There was no lawman to turn them over to. They ought to be shot, but gunshots would arouse the neighbors and they'd be pounding on Mary's door. He wanted to kill them. He hated them. What they had tried to do was worse than murder. Murder happened all the time, but not rape. An assault against a woman was the most despicable crime a man could commit. They didn't deserve to live. The world would be better off without them. Shooting them would be doing the world a favor. Tom aimed his gun at Sam'l and his finger tightened on the trigger.

"Tom," Mary said. "Tom, don't."

She was right. He forced himself to relax. He couldn't just kill them. He had to let them go. What else could he do?

"Get out," he said. "On your feet, both of you. Out the front door. Come back here and I'll blow your goddamn heads off. Get up and get the hell out of here."

"Thanks, Cap'n," Sam'l said. They got to their feet and walked to the front door. Two guns were on the kitchen floor—Tom's and the one belonging to Job. Both men were unarmed now. "This is the second time you coulda killed me." Sam'l opened the door, looked out.

"Get."

They left.

She shot the bolt in the door and was in his arms. He held her tight and put his face in her hair. Now that the danger was over, she couldn't hold back the tears and she cried softly against his shoulder. He held her and let her cry.

When she looked up at him, she let out a groan. "Oh, Tom. Tom, you're hurt." Her fingers moved over his face and came away bloody. He grinned a weak grin. "Doesn't feel like much. Probably a scalp cut."

"Come on." She led him by the arm back to the kitchen and got him seated. "Let's have a look." She turned up the lamp that was lit and held it close. "I see two cuts. Still bleeding. He must have hit you with a gun butt."

Grinning, Tom said, "Well, it sure wasn't with his finger."

"What can we do? We have to do something."

"Not much we can do. It'll stop bleeding pretty soon."

"No, let's clean the wounds. I'll heat some water."

"I'm all right, Mary. Are you all right?"

"Yes, I'm..." Suddenly her legs went weak and she sat down hard in a kitchen chair. She put her face in her hands and cried softly again.

Shannon went to her and put an arm around her shoulders. "Go ahead and cry, Mary. What happened was, well, it was hell, that's what it was. You held up very well, Mary." His voice was soft, soothing. "Most women—men too—would have just broke up in little pieces. You were wonderful, Mary."

Tears were in her eyes when she looked up at him. "At first, when they grabbed me and held their hands over my mouth, I was glad you were coming and then I was afraid for you. They had seen you and knew you were coming in the back door and—"

113

"Mary, Mary. Just relax. It's over now. They're gone and they won't be back."

She wiped her eyes with the palms of her hands. "I'm sorry, Tom. You're the one who was hurt, not me."

He chuckled without humor. "I'll tell you one thing, I'm getting a lot of experience snatching guns out of men's hands. This was the second—no, the third—time I got away from men with guns. Three times in the past seven or eight days. If you hadn't jumped on that jasper named Job I'd be dead."

"Sit down, please, and let me do whatever I can for you." She got up and busied herself building a fire in the cookstove, then she pumped a pot of water.

CHAPTER 21

The cuts on Tom Shannon's head stopped bleeding, but Mary was worried. "You need a doctor, but there's no such thing in Fortune."

"I'll just have to survive without a doctor."

"Does it still hurt?"

"A little."

"I've read about head injuries. You could have a concussion and not know it. Sometimes people suffering a concussion feel all right for a while, then feel gosh-awful later."

"I've been hit on the head before," he said, remembering the fight he'd had at Tarryall. "I'm not going to let this kill me, not after everything else that's happened."

"We don't even have a way of keeping it clean."

"I'll keep my hat on. That way no dirt can get in it."

"Oh, Tom." She sat on his lap again. "What are we going to do?"

Sadly, he said, "I don't know. I got Zack Parmell to answer a lot of questions, but I didn't learn anything useful."

"I'm still asking questions. And that reminds me, Zack Parmell came into the Silver Lode and got me aside and told me about meeting you up in the hills. He said to tell you he won't tell anyone about it."

"I'm surprised. He was on the jury that convicted me."

"Yes, I remember, and I asked him about that. He said he'd

been thinking it over and now he has a—what did he call it?—a reasonable doubt."

"Well, I don't know how much help he can be, but I'd rather have him for a friend than an enemy. He did say Scott Wheeler and his dad didn't get along too good. Said they argued a lot and had a big yelling match just before V.C. came to town and ran into me. That explains why they didn't speak to each other in the Salty Dog, but I don't see how that can explain anything else."

She got off his lap and sat in another chair. "I keep asking everyone I know who was in the saloon that night, and they all say you were the only one Scott Wheeler had any trouble with. Except the sheepherder, of course, and he couldn't have done it."

"Someone did it and he had a reason, and someone else knows about it."

"All I hear is that the hooligans are organized. That's what everyone thinks now. They seem to know everything that goes on, when money or gold is on the stage or being sent by a messenger, when the sawmill is ready to pay the workers, when anyone collects enough gold dust or nuggets to make it worth their while to rob him. They knew when the Running W crew was up in the hills gathering cattle and no one was at the ranch to stop them from stealing cattle. They knew when Deputy Atwell was taking Orville with him and going northeast to try to track you down, and they knew when and where to ambush him."

Tom's lips turned up in a grim smile; "If Atwell hadn't had Orville with him, and if Orville hadn't got a glimpse of the killer, everyone would think I did it."

"Yes. Orville was very happy to be alive after that."

"Could Orville...? Naw."

"No," she said quickly. "Not Orville."

"All right. But someone around here is sure keeping his eyes and ears open. And the gang has to have somebody with good eyes and ears in the bank at Fairplay and at Tarryall. They had someone in the bank here too, because they knew when the bank had enough cash on hand worth stealing."

"They're organized, all right."

"Damn. Wish we had some law around here. We could have

116

turned those two would-be rapers over to the law, and maybe they'd have spilled something."

"Do you think they're part of the gang?"

"I know they are. The one named Sam'l is one of the two I fought with up there. They were on their way somewhere then. Probably to meet with others and rustle some Running W cattle. And, come to think of it, one of them said something about... Let me think. He said something about how someone wouldn't like it if they didn't show up when they were supposed to. I didn't think much of it then. I had too many other things to think about. But now...hmmm. Someone planned the whole thing and they were taking orders from him." Tom pounded his knee with a fist. "Some damn body is doing the thinking for the gang, and I'll bet it's someone here in town."

"Yes." Her face was alive now." And whoever it is planned the murder of Scott Wheeler."

"Yeah, but..." He shrugged. "Who?"

Mary was getting excited. "Now that we've figured out this much...now that we know it's someone in Fortune, I can ask more-intelligent questions of the men who come into the cafe. Eventually, Tom, we're going to solve this puzzle."

"Uh-huh." He tried to share in her excitement, couldn't. "What then? We'd have to prove it, and to do that I'd have to show myself, and if I did that I'd be shot or hung."

"But we've figured out this much, and we can figure out the rest. Maybe something will happen in our favor. A gang member could be wounded and would tell all to save his own skin. Something could happen."

"Could be. But I can't wait for a miracle. I need to do something now. I'm getting damned tired of this way of living, and the longer I hang around here the more likely it is that someone will see me, someone who will tell."

"We, Tom. *We* need to do something."

They fell silent. Shannon rolled a cigarette, lit it, smoked, then said, "All right, we've decided that someone in Fortune is doing the thinking. It has to be someone who's in a position to know everything that's going on. Who could that be?"

She sighed. "Who? Let's see. There's C.H. Tibalt at the Fortune

Mercantile. He hears everything."

"Yeah. And the mercantile has never been robbed. In fact, I met a string of his freight wagons heading east a few days ago, and the teamsters had rifles, but no outriders. They had to have had some money with them to pay for supplies; but they didn't seem to be afraid of being robbed."

"The mercantile has not been robbed, and neither has the hardware store nor the blacksmith nor the laundry nor the Fortune Hotel. Mr. March at the hardware has guns of all kinds for sale, and bullets, as well as mining tools and saws and things. Outlaws need guns and bullets."

"Could March or Tibalt be the one? Or both?"

She shook her head. "That would be hard to believe. The way they talk, they want to get rid of the hooligans more than anyone else. Except me, of course."

"Yeah. They've got money invested here. A ghost town is no place to invest money."

"It could be."

He exhaled a lungful of smoke. "What do you mean?"

"I mean, well, I didn't mean to change the subject, but people are leaving Fortune, and if things go on this way the town will be a ghost town as you said, and, uh, I've been thinking."

"Yeah?" He was studying her face.

"It could be a good place to invest in real estate. I've been reading about real estate investments, and, well, right now you can buy a house and lot in Fortune for a song. I mean, people are leaving and are more than happy to sell their property for whatever they can get."

"Yeah, I know."

"Look at it this way: You've got a little money. Not much, but a little. Suppose you were to buy a house and lot and the town survived? I mean, suppose the hoodlums are caught and prosecuted, or scared off, and the town becomes a safe place to work and do business? People would come back. They'd be looking for houses and lots. You could double, even triple, your investment."

He stared at her, unbelieving. "You mean you're thinking about investments while I'm thinking about how to keep on living?"

A long sigh came out of her. "It's wicked of me, I suppose. But I've been reading about all the people who got rich by investing in real estate, and it occurred to me that here is an opportunity."

He continued staring at her.

"Law and order will come to Fortune. It's inevitable. Maybe not this year, but it will come. Congress is going to make Colorado a state, and Fortune will one day be incorporated and it will have a government and a marshal, and it will grow."

He shrugged. "Well, I reckon that's one of the differences between people who get rich and people who spend their lives working their hearts out for nothing. The rich ones are always thinking about ways to make money, and the poor ones are always thinking about where their next meal is coming from."

"That's exactly right, Tom. Am I wicked to be thinking about investments?"

"Naw. I reckon not."

"I know a family that's leaving Fortune, and they have a four-room house, a stable, and a lot that takes in half a block. The man was in the Silver Lode only this morning, moaning because he couldn't sell his property. If you paid him anything at all for it, you'd be doing him a favor."

"Me? How...?"

"I can arrange it. I can get him to sign the deed over to you. I'll just tell everyone that I believe in you and I believe you'll come back to Fortune, and now that your cabin has been burned down you'll need a place to live."

Shaking his head, Tom mulled it over. Then slowly, almost reluctantly, he reached into the pocket of his cotton duck pants and produced his roll of bills. "There's not much here. I had to buy a horse and some supplies. But"—he shrugged again—"I won't be needing any money, living the way I am."

"I'll lend you the rest. I have a little money. You can pay me back when this is over and you can sell a few calves or something."

He chuckled a dry chuckle. "A house and lot in Fortune isn't worth more than a few head of livestock, huh?"

"No, it really isn't."

"Well, all this doesn't solve my, our, problem. And"—he

119

chuckled again—"now that I'm about to be a property owner, I have to solve it."

"Let's go to bed."

"Now? I—"

"I'm not having any romantic notions, not after what happened tonight. It's just that you need rest. I'll feel a lot better about you if you're not seeing double or having a lapse of memory by morning."

"Maybe you're right." He stood up wearily, went into the bedroom, sat on the bed, and pulled off his boots.

CHAPTER 22

It was the sound of a chair leg scraping the floor that woke him up. He sat up immediately and groped for Mary's side of the bed. She wasn't there. A lamp was burning in the kitchen, but outside the window it was still dark. Hastily, he reached for his shirt and couldn't find it. His pants were on a chair beside the bed, but not his shirt. Then Mary came into the room, smiling, and he breathed a heavy sigh of relief. "Your shirt is drying. It was all bloody and I washed it."

"Oh, uh, thanks."

"I want you to have a good meal this morning, darling. It will be ready soon."

"Yeah." He grinned. "Eat and run."

"Better to have you for a few hours than not at all."

A dull pain still pounded inside his head, but it was less severe than it had been before he went to sleep. "I'm not seeing double and I remember everything that happened," he said.

"Thank God. I was worried."

"Maybe reading all those doctor books makes you worry too much."

"That could be, but you know how I like to read."

He washed his face in a pan of water she had warmed on the stove and dried himself with a towel made from a flour sack. Breakfast was just what he needed; bacon, hot biscuits, blackstrap molasses, and coffee. Two cups of coffee. When he finished, he put his hat on carefully and was pleasantly surprised to find it didn't come into contact with the cuts on top of his head. Ready to leave now, he said, "I can't keep sneaking over here in the night. Someone is bound to get suspicious."

"If you don't come, I'll worry. I'll worry anyway, but if I don't see you tonight I'll worry more."

"All right, I'll try. But if I don't show up, don't worry too much. If anything happens to me you'll probably hear about it in the Silver Lode Cafe."

"You know I'll worry."

"Blow out the light, will you, and don't light it again until I'm horseback and on my way."

"Tom." She put her arms around his neck and kissed him soundly on the mouth. "Please come back tonight."

"All right. I'll be here."

The sorrel horse was glad to get back to camp, get the saddle off and graze, but to Tom the camp was a dismal place. It was cloudy again and it looked as if the first snow of the season was just ahead. The clouds were so low he couldn't see the tops of the hills surrounding his camp. He wrapped himself in a blanket and walked around, stomping his feet and cursing.

"Damn, damn, damn." Never had he felt so helpless and frustrated. Not even when the war ended and he knew his side had lost, knew all those good men had died for nothing.

The cuts on his head stung, but he had noted with satisfaction the night before that the bullet wound in his left side was healing. What a sorry mess I am, he thought. Shot in the side, beat over the head twice, beard like a hermit. How can Mary stand me? Hell, I can't stand myself. He sat on the ground and leaned back against a rock. What to do? Damn.

What would a detective do? Hell, I don't know. Ask questions, I reckon. Ask questions and maybe get a little bit of information out of everyone and put it together. Who to ask? If he could move around and be seen without being shot, he could ask questions of everyone who'd known Scott Wheeler and everyone who'd been in the Salty Dog that night. He could ask questions of the merchants and the robbery victims and even V.C. Wheeler. Someone knew something. A gang that busy has to let something slip once in a while.

V.C. Wheeler? He didn't get along with his only offspring, but he didn't shoot him. Tom snorted. Thinks I shot him. Still, he knew his son better than anyone else. Might remember something that could help. What's the difference? He wouldn't talk to me. He wouldn't tell me the way out of a timber fire.

Have to talk to him, though. He's the only possibility. Tibalt at the mercantile probably knows nothing, and neither does Hugh March at the hardware store. Or do they? They know they haven't been robbed, and they are probably thinking the same thing I am: they haven't been robbed because the gang needs supplies. That means gang members come into their stores. Wouldn't they be a little suspicious when a man came in and bought supplies for five or six men? Ought to be. Especially Tibalt. Might be a good idea to question that gentleman too.

There was only one way to do it. He would visit Mary as soon as she got home, then visit C.H. Tibalt. The merchants closed their stores an hour earlier than the Silver Lode Cafe closed, so he'd have to go to Tibalt's house. Let's see, C.H. Tibalt lives alone with his wife. A middle-aged couple with no children. He was fat and moved slow. Shannon couldn't remember ever seeing Mrs. Tibalt, and he wasn't sure where the couple lived. Mary would know. He'd have to go and knock on their door and put a gun in Tibalt's face and force him to answer some questions. After that, Tom's life would be in even more jeopardy. Unlike Zack Parmell, Tibalt would tell. The town would know that Tom Shannon was back, and was sneaking around in the dark, asking questions. Tom would be hunted again.

Well, there was no other way.

He ate a cold lunch, afraid to build a fire. Smoke could be seen even on an overcast day. He moved his horse from a grazing spot in the open to another spot under some spruce where the grass was belly high. Twice, he had to untie the animal and unwrap the picket rope from around a tree. At midafternoon the horse lay down to rest. Tom, wrapped in his blankets, dozed too.

At sundown the weather turned worse. What had started as a misty rain turned to snow. Big fat flakes of snow. That's just dandy,

Tom thought bitterly. Snow makes tracking easy. Now it would be impossible to shake off any pursuers. He could only hope that the earth was still warm enough to melt the snow as it fell, or that it would continue snowing and cover his tracks long after he left town and was well up in the hills again.

It did neither.

By dark the snow was sticking to the ground and had accumulated enough that he couldn't move without leaving tracks. Then it quit.

Shannon cursed his luck. Sometimes a man just can't win for losing, he thought. He saddled his horse, rolled up his camp, and left the roll under a tall spruce. He mounted and rode in the dark down out of the mountains onto the high plains toward the town of Fortune. The sky was still overcast and there was no light from the moon or stars. "Good thing you can see in the dark, old horse," Tom said, "because I sure as hell can't."

The horse carried him to the Ute Trail road, and he followed it to the outskirts of town, then took a roundabout route to Mary's house. How he envied the people he could see through the windows. Eating a hot supper, going to a warm dry bed, not worried about a knock on the door and having to face men with guns who wanted to hang them. Damn, he grumbled. Damn it all anyway. How did the outlaws stand living the way they did? Hiding out in the hills, always being hunted. If he were an outlaw, Shannon decided, he'd head for a warmer climate in the winter. Or for some big city where he could live high and spend all the money he'd stolen during the summer. He sure wouldn't hang around Fortune.

Mary was already at home. A lamp illuminated the kitchen, and he could see her moving shadow. He tied his horse inside the backyard fence and knocked lightly on the kitchen door. Immediately, the light went out and the door opened. She spoke his name, and he stepped inside. After a long embrace she pulled the heavy curtains closed over the window and lit the lamp again. To Tom, she was beautiful. He appreciated the way she parted her brown hair on the side and let it hang down, but leaving it fluffed up enough that it wasn't slicked down. And there were her wide gray eyes, straight nose, and firm, full mouth. Seeing her caused an ache in his chest and made him feel sad instead of happy. Would they ever be allowed to live a normal life?

She got him to sit down, and stood over him, parting his hair and examining the wounds on his head. "Scabbed over. That's good."

"I'll live." Then he said, "I'm going to do something tonight, Mary, that might be foolish, but I've got to do something."

"What, darling?"

"Try to talk to C.H. Tibalt. We know the gang is buying supplies from him. He might know something useful."

"Huh-uh." She shook her head. "You wouldn't get within a mile of him now. He was robbed last night."

"What?" Tom's hand paused in midair as he started to light a smoke.

"It was the same two that were here last night. They wore those black rags, but he described them perfectly. Everyone figures they went first to Mr. March's hardware store, broke open the back door, and helped themselves to some guns, then went to Mr. Tibalt's house and robbed him, and, uh...Mr. Tibalt isn't saying so, but we think they, uh, well, he sent his wife to Fairplay on the stage today. He won't talk about it. They said Mrs. Tibalt wouldn't speak to anyone when she got on the stage."

"Aw, hell. Is anyone doing anything about it?"

"No. Not a thing. The stage driver promised to notify the marshal in Fairplay, but he won't get here until tomorrow sometime. If he comes at all. Nothing will be done."

Shannon's voice was bitter. "They can just rob and murder and loot and rape all they want to and nobody does anything."

"There's no leadership, Tom. Ever since Deputy Atwell was shot down, no one wants to take over and try to organize the townsmen."

Frowning at the floor, Shannon said, "Because I let them go instead of shooting them down when I had a chance, someone else was robbed and a woman was raped."

"There's a lesson in that. But letting them go was my idea. I'm to blame."

"If I were Tibalt, I'd be so damned mad I'd go after them by myself if I had to." Tom lit his cigarette with angry, jerky movements, blew smoke. Then he said, "No, I probably wouldn't. That would be suicide. Getting killed won't solve anything."

"That's what he said."

"I'd still like to talk to him. He just might know something that would help identify the rest of them, or help find their hideout, or—"

"He'd shoot you on sight."

"Yeah." Glumly.

Mary went to the stove, opened the oven, and released a delicious odor. "I've got another roast cooking. Mr. Tibalt managed to buy some fresh-butchered beef yesterday before everything happened, and I bought five pounds of rump roast. I think it's ready to eat."

They ate. Roast beef, boiled potatoes, gravy, and fresh bread. "He asked me why I was buying so much, and I couldn't think of a quick lie, so I just didn't answer."

"He's got other things to think about now," Tom allowed between bites.

"Tom." Mary put down her knife and fork and looked across the table at him. "Maybe I could approach him. He trusts me. If I could get close enough to his door and speak to him through the door, maybe he'd open it for me."

He stopped chewing long enough to mull it over. "He'd think you were crazy. Why would you be knocking on his door at night? Why would you even be out at night?"

"Yes, you're right." She resumed eating. "He'd know something was very strange and he'd be doubly careful."

As good as the meal was, Shannon wasn't enjoying himself. He chewed slowly, thoughtfully. Worry wrinkles crossed his forehead. When he cleaned his plate he rolled another smoke and lit it by holding one end over the lamp globe and drawing on the other end. Mary scraped and stacked the dishes beside the sink, put a pot of water on to heat.

"I've just got to do something, Mary. I, we, can't go on this way forever." He smoked. "I just don't know what to do."

She sat across the table. "Do you really think Mr. Tibalt might know something helpful?"

"It's possible."

"All right, let's go talk to him."

"How? He's armed and ready for anything and he's got blood in his eye."

"I'll go with you and call to him. Maybe I can coax him out, or at least to the door."

"And then I'll have to put a gun on him and question him at gunpoint."

She sighed. "It's the only way I can think of."

"And he'll be mad at you too."

"Yes, but he won't do anything about it. He's no killer and there's no one around to arrest me. Of course..." Her hands twitched nervously on the table. "He'll know you've been coming here at night. Everyone will know, and you won't be able to come here anymore. I'm not sure I could stand that."

"Yeah." He snubbed out his cigarette and rolled another. "I guess it's a bad idea, but...dammit, I can't keep sneaking over here at night. This whole thing has got to come to a head one way or another."

He stood. "I've just got to do something."

"All right. Let me get my coat. I'll wash the dishes later."

CHAPTER 23

They walked in the dark with Tom leading his horse to the home of C.H. Tibalt four blocks away. They circled the house and found that the store owner had a small stable and corral at the back of his house. Tom tied his horse there, then they went cautiously in the dark to the front door. They paused. There was lamplight in the house. Tibalt was at home. Mary whispered, "Here I go," and Tom gave her hand a squeeze. She walked with bold steps to the door.

"Mr. Tibalt." No answer. Louder, "Mr. Tibalt, it's Mary Cress." Still no answer, though they saw a shadow move past a window. "Mr. Tibalt, it's Mary Cress. I need to talk to you."

Finally, the door opened a crack. "Mrs. Cress? Mary?"

"Yes, Mr. Tibalt. I need to talk to you about something important." She moved in front of the door where she could be seen in the light that spilled out. Tom stood flattened against the side of the house next to the door.

"What in tarnation is it, Mary? What in thunderation brings you out here at night?"

"Mr. Tibalt, those men who robbed you last night, I didn't tell anyone, but they came to my house too."

"Oh, my God. Did they hurt you?"

"No, Mr. Tibalt. I had a friend with me. Between the two of us we fought them off."

The door opened wider. "A friend? Who was that?" C.H. Tibalt's overweight frame filled the door, and he had a six-gun in his hand. His gun hand hung loosely at his side.

Tom had his own gun ready. He moved fast, jumping between Tibalt and Mary. He grabbed the man's gun hand before he could bring the gun up. Tibalt staggered back into the room with Tom following, hanging onto the gun hand. Tom pointed his own gun at Tibalt's face.

"Stop. Stand still, Mr. Tibalt. I won't hurt you if you'll just stand still."

The store owner's eyes were wide, fixed on Shannon's gun. He allowed his own gun to be twisted from his hand. His mouth opened and closed and a strangling sound came from his throat.

"I'm real sorry, sir," Tom said, "but I need to talk with you."

"Mr. Tibalt," Mary said, "we mean you no harm. I'm sorry I had to fool you this way."

Tibalt choked, gasped, and spoke in a strangled voice, "Why, you, you're...you're Tom Shannon."

"Yes sir, Mr. Tibalt. Will you sit down, please? I only want to ask you some questions."

The store owner took three steps backward and sat heavily on a short stuffed sofa. Tom, with two guns in his hands, stood before him. Mary was behind Tom. She closed the door.

"What...what do you want?"

"I was hoping, Mr. Tibalt, that you might know something that would help me prove I didn't kill Scott Wheeler."

"How...how would I know anything?"

Shannon squatted on his heels. Mary stood behind him, clasping her hands nervously in front of her.

"You have the only mercantile in town, Mr. Tibalt, and everyone believes—knows—that the gang of robbers is holed up somewhere around here. They have to buy supplies from you. I was hoping that you might have seen something or heard something that would help identify them or find them."

The fat merchant began shaking his head immediately. "No. I know nothing."

"Are you sure?" Tom squinted at him. "We think there has to be six or eight of them. They use a lot of groceries. Who buys that many groceries?"

"Uh, a lot of people."

"Who?"

"Well"—Tibalt licked his lips—"there are timber camps and mining camps. Great Northern has a timber camp five miles from here. You ought to know that, you worked for them."

"Yeah." Tom pondered that, then said, "You knew that, and you know just about everything that goes on around here. Who that you don't know buys a lot of groceries at a time?"

"Now see here." The fat man was regaining his composure. "I don't have to answer to you."

"No, Mr. Tibalt," Tom said with resignation, "you don't. I was just hoping you would want to help rid this town of the gang that robbed you."

"Of course I do. But what has all this got to do with the murder of Scott Wheeler?"

Shannon shook his head. "I don't know. Maybe nothing. We think his murder was planned by someone who wanted him dead for some reason or other, and whoever it was made it look like I did it. It might have something to do with all the robberies and murders around here."

Mary spoke up. "We're desperate, Mr. Tibalt. We're grabbing at every possibility."

"It could be," Shannon said, "that the gang considered Wheeler a threat to them."

"But all the evidence pointed to you."

"Sure, sure. But I know—and Mary knows—I didn't do it. That means someone else did, and we're thinking the whole scheme is tied to everything else that's been going on."

"Well"—the fat man wiped a hand across his mouth—"all I know is what I heard at the trial."

"Think, Mr. Tibalt," Mary pleaded. "Think about everyone who came into the store, everyone you didn't know. Try to remember what they did and what they said."

"Those two who robbed you last night, did they ever come into your store?"

"Well, not that I recollect. That one that wore a cap, I've heard about him. He was in on some of the robberies and shootings. That cap isn't easy to forget. But I never saw him in the store."

"He'd change caps. They'd change clothes, horses, and everything else. That means they've got a hideout someplace where they can keep horses and supplies."

Tibalt was quiet, pulling at his double chin with a thumb and forefinger. Mary shuffled her feet nervously. Tom stayed in his squatting position. One gun was on the floor between his feet and the other was in his hand.

"There was this one feller," Tibalt said, and paused.

"Yeah?"

"Everybody else hauled their goods away in wagons, but this one brought two packhorses. The first time, I helped him load the panniers and hang them on the pack saddles, and I ask him who he was keeping camp for, and he said he was packing for a bunch of timber cutters."

"Uh-huh. Did he say where his camp was?"

"Well, he said it was north, but when he left town he went east on the Ute road."

"Ever see him again?"

"Yeah. Several times. I saw him coming out of the Salty Dog once and I saw him in the Silver Lode Cafe. In fact, Mary, you waited on him. He was a chunky kind of feller, not as fat as me, but heavy-like with a trimmed beard. He paid in cash."

"I'm not..." Mary's face screwed up as she tried to remember. "I waited on so many men, I don't..."

"Did he come into the store more than once?"

"Twice. Last time he had the same two packhorses. I ask him again where he was taking the groceries, and that time he said he was cooking for a cattle-gathering crew over on the Tarryall River. He was lying, and he didn't remember from one trip to the next what lie he'd told."

"Did he go east again?"

"Yep. I watched him out of curiosity."

"Hmmm."

"They're up there somewhere," Mary said.

"Yeah," said Tom. "East. Their hideout is someplace where they can't pull a wagon. That means north in the mountains. East, then north."

"There's a lot of territory up there," said Tibalt.

Shannon asked more questions, but learned nothing interesting. Then it was time to go. He picked up the fat man's gun, flipped open the loading gate, and dumped the cartridges out one at a time. He put the cartridges in his shirt pocket.

"I'll leave your gun empty, Mr. Tibalt. You've probably got a rifle in the house too, but I'll be gone in the dark before you can get outside after me. Mary is going home. I don't want you to bother her. She didn't hurt you and I didn't hurt you and you'd just better not bother her. If you do, I'll be back and I'll be looking for you." Tom's mouth turned down, making a bitter face. "I'm a killer, you know."

Taking Mary by the arm, he backed to the door. Then they were out of the house, half-running to the back yard where he located his horse and prepared to mount.

In a whisper, he said, "I don't know when I'll see you again, Mary. I'll be back. I don't know when, but I'll be back."

She whispered, "Be careful, Tom. I lost one man. I don't want to lose you too."

"I'll be careful."

"I love you, Tom."

"I love you too, Mary."

He mounted and rode away at a gallop, heading east.

CHAPTER 24

Two miles out of town he stopped and listened. He heard no pursuers. Riding at a trot now, he continued east four miles then turned south onto the plains. A wagon road led to the Running W Ranch, he knew, but he couldn't see it in the dark. Snow began falling again and he didn't care. It was so dark he could barely see his horse's head, and he could only hope he was going in the right direction.

On he went, standing in his stirrups at times to make the jarring trotting gait more comfortable. When the sorrel horse stopped suddenly, he guessed they had come to the Running W's wire-fenced horse pasture.

"Good thing you saw it, old feller, because I sure didn't," he said aloud. The ranch headquarters couldn't be more than two miles from there. Ought to be a light of some kind on. He reined the horse to the left, going east, and followed the fence two miles, then continued following it where it turned south. After another half-mile he topped a rise and stopped again. Below him, in a shallow valley, he could see a dark blob, a shade darker than the rest of the night, which he guessed were the ranch buildings and a grove of cottonwood trees growing along a creek. He urged his mount on at a walk, approaching the buildings carefully. When the sorrel stopped again, he knew he had come to a cross fence.

"Dammit," he whispered to himself, "where's the damn gate? There's got to be a gate." He dismounted, found the wire fence with his hands. "It's just a guess," he whispered, "but I'm guessing the gate is closer to the buildings." He followed the fence, keeping his hands on it, walking and leading the horse.

"Darker than a stack of black cats."

Five hundred yards on, his hand collided with a wooden post that was bigger around and taller than the others. Groping blindly, he found the two wire loops that held a wire gate closed, and lifted the gate stick out of the loops. He led his horse through the gate and closed it. Mounted, he rode toward the dark blob of buildings, and as he got closer he could see a light in a window. Then another light in another window.

Soon he was near a large dark building which he guessed was a barn, and there he dismounted again. Still working by feel, he found a corral and he tied his horse to a corral post. He used a slip knot, believing he'd have to leave in a hurry.

Now he looked carefully back the way he'd come, trying to find a landmark, something that would make it easier to find the pasture gate again. The darkness hid all landmarks. He put his back to the corral and faced the way he'd come. A little to the right and I ought to find it, he thought.

Now comes the tricky part.

Tom Shannon crawled between the corral poles, crossed the corral, and crawled out the other side. He walked as quietly as he could toward one of the lighted windows. A dog barked. Shannon stopped, stood perfectly still. He heard the dog coming in the dark. He breathed a sigh of relief when the animal's cold nose touched his hand. "Good boy," he whispered, reaching down and scratching a shaggy body. A friendly dog. Had to be friendly on a ranch where ranch hands came and went.

By now he was close enough to the lighted window to see it was a bunkhouse. He dropped to the ground when the door opened and a man came out. The man closed the door behind him, and soon Tom could hear him relieving his bladder onto the ground. When he went back inside, Tom heard him say, "Snowin, and darker'n old Coalie's ass out there." The door was closed.

All right, if this was the bunkhouse, then the other light had to be in the main house where V.C. Wheeler lived. Tom crept on, ignoring the falling snow. When he got close enough to the window to see in, he saw Wheeler sitting in a big stuffed chair reading a book. A lamp was on a small table beside the chair.

Enough light came from the window that Tom could find the front door, and now he walked heavily as he stepped onto a wooden porch and crossed it. He knocked on the door.

"Who's there?"

In a voice purposely muffled, Tom said, "It's me, Mr. Wheeler."

"Who?"

"It's me." Again in a muffled voice.

The door opened. Tom stepped in front of Wheeler and shoved him hard, sending him stumbling back into the room. Tom followed with his gun in his hand. "Don't move," he hissed. "Move and you're dead." He reached back and shut the door.

Wheeler's thick gray eyebrows pulled together in an angry frown, but he didn't speak. His suspenders hung down over his baggy wool pants and his plump stomach showed between the buttons of his undershirt.

"Get away from the window. I mean it, Wheeler."

The stout rancher stepped away from the window, farther back into the room.

"Sit down over there." Shannon motioned with the gun toward a wooden chair against a far wall.

Finally, Wheeler spoke. "Who the hell are you? What the hell do you want?" Then recognition came. "Tom Shannon. What the hell do you want, Shannon?"

"Answers," Tom hissed. "Keep your voice down or you won't live long enough to give me any answers. I'm a damned killer, you know."

"Yeah," Wheeler said, sitting in a chair, "I know."

"You don't know a damn thing, Wheeler." Shannon moved around beside him to a spot in the shadows. "I didn't kill your damn son. Plenty of other men could have killed him. Fact is, I heard you didn't get along with him too good yourself."

"I wouldn't shoot my own son."

"No, but you might know something that would help me find out who did."

"What the hell do you mean, find out who did? You did. It was proven in a court of law."

"That jury was too damned bloodthirsty. They wanted to hang someone. I happened to be handy."

"You had a fair trial."

"I don't think so. Now, I want you to tell me everything that happened the day before Scott Wheeler was killed."

"Why should I tell you anything? Besides, if I knew anything I'd have told the jury."

"You might know something important without realizing it. I want to hear about everything that happened."

"Nothing happened. And why should I tell you anything anyway?"

"Because, Mr. Wheeler"—Tom's voice was low, menacing—"I'm getting damned tired of running and hiding in the dark, and I'm either going to find out who really killed your kid or I'm going to die trying. And I'll tell you something else: If I go down, I just might take some of you godamighty yahoos down with me."

"Nothing happened."

"The hell it didn't. You and your kid had a hell of an argument. You were so mad at each other you didn't even speak when you saw each other in the Salty Dog."

"That's none of your business."

"Every damned thing that happened is my business."

V.C. Wheeler sat up straighter in his chair. His eyes were on the gun in Tom's hand. "I'm telling you, Shannon, I don't know anything that would help you. I'll say it again: If I knew anything I would have told the jury."

"What did Scott do that day?"

"He hung around the ranch, fixing his saddle and braiding some hobbles."

"He practiced with his gun, didn't he?"

"Yeah. So what?"

"Never mind. What did he do the day before that and the day before that?"

"The day before that he rode a big circle up there, pushing Running W cattle down."

"Was he by himself?"

"He started out with a crew of about five men, but they split up."

"Did he see anything unusual?"

"I don't know. I didn't ask him."

"How about the day before that?"

"The day before that? I don't know."

"Yes, you do. You know."

"All right, he did the same thing. We were gathering cattle out of the high hills."

"Did he see anything? Come on, you two had supper together and you surely talked to each other once in a while."

"Listen, Shannon, hand me the gun. I'll see that you get a new trial and I'll see you have ample time to prepare your defense."

"Why didn't you see to that the first time?"

A long sigh came out of the stout rancher. "All right, I'll admit I was angry. My only son had been shot in the back. All evidence pointed to you."

"Oh, I see." A sneer crept into Tom's voice. "And now you're having second thoughts."

"Tell me something, Shannon. Did you come here to rob me?"

"No. I never robbed anyone in my life. And I never killed anyone except in the war. And even then I didn't shoot anyone who wasn't shooting at me."

"All right, I'm not sure I believe you, but I'm willing to use all my influence to get you a new trial. You can even have the trial moved to Fairplay."

"A week ago that would have sounded mighty good to me, Wheeler, but now I'm damned mad. I not only want to prove myself innocent, I want to know who did kill your son."

"And you think I might be able to help you."

"I'm just hoping."

"Hmmm." The rancher scratched his jaw and studied the floor. "If I knew anything I'd tell you."

"I'll ask you again, did Scott mention anything out of the ordinary at any time?"

"All he said was he saw that gambler, that faro dealer from the

Salty Dog saloon, up there to the north."

"Is that all?"

"Well, they stopped and talked a bit. He said the gambler—what's his name?—was elk hunting and hadn't seen any."

"That's all?"

Wheeler scratched his jaw again and shook his head. "That's all. Except the cattle were fat from that mountain grass, and we'd have some good beef to sell." A scowl crossed Wheeler's face. "But the thieves beat us to it."

It occurred to Shannon that this was the second time in a few hours that he had questioned someone at the point of a gun. It was the third time in the past few days he'd pointed a gun at someone and asked questions. First, Zack Parmell, then C.H. Tibalt, and now Wheeler. Suddenly he was very tired, and he drew in a long breath and let it out slowly. He saw Wheeler's eyes narrow.

"What are you going to do, kill me? How do you think you're going to get away from here? I've got five armed men in the bunkhouse."

"No, Wheeler, I'm not going to kill you unless I have to. How am I going to get away? Well, I'll tell you. I've got a horse tied on the other side of a corral. You're going out there with me. I'll hang onto you, and if you make a noise or try to run I'll put a bullet in you."

The rancher said no more. Tom added with sarcasm, "I'm a killer, you know."

He ordered the rancher to stand and turn around. He got hold of his drooping suspenders. "Now blow out the light and go to the door. Move slow." He held the gun against the rancher's back, then changed his mind and held it a few inches away from him. No use showing his enemy exactly where the gun was and inviting him to try to spin around and grab it.

With Wheeler in front of him, Tom made his way past the bunkhouse, past the curious but friendly dog, and to the corrals. "Crawl through and don't try to pull away from me." They got to the horse. He untied the horse and mounted.

He spoke, his voice barely above a whisper. "I've been thinking, Wheeler. When I came here I stopped a few days in Pueblo. That's where I bought my cows and bulls. The man I bought them from runs a slaughterhouse and doesn't care who he buys cattle from. It's too late to get your beeves back. They've been slaughtered and their hides burned or buried by now. But the next time someone steals cattle around here, that's a place to look."

Wheeler spoke for the first time since they had left the house. His voice was gruff but not unfriendly. "I'll keep that in mind."

Without another word, Shannon reined his horse around and rode away in the dark. It was still snowing and the cold wet flakes touched his face.

CHAPTER 25

He found the gate, but only after walking and leading his horse for a hundred yards and groping for it. An hour later he was in the foothills and climbing steadily. He allowed the horse to walk in the steep places, but kept it moving until he came to a hill that he guessed was so steep and so high that climbing it would tire the animal too much. He unsaddled and made a hobble by rolling up his jacket and tying knots in it. With the horse's front feet hobbled and still wearing the bridle, it could graze and rest but not travel.

The snow came down in big flakes, but up here it wasn't so wet. He silently thanked the lodgepole pines for the branches that always died and dried up on the lower sections, and he broke off some and got a warming fire going.

At daylight he was on horseback again, climbing higher and heading north and east. By noon he came to the spot where he had eaten a raven and where he had left the dead body of an outlaw. The body was gone. An hour later the snow stopped, but by now the ground was covered with six inches of it. After climbing to the top of a long ridge, he stayed on top and kept his horse traveling at a steady mile-eating trot until he looked down and saw the sheep.

The old herder smiled widely when he saw who was coming, and Tom rode up, dismounted, and shook hands with him.

"Moving out of all this snow?"

"Yep. Should have moved a week ago."

"Where's your wagon?"

"Back yonder. I can't drive a team and handle these little woolly brutes at the same time. I hired a kid from town to bring the wagon down."

"I'd help you, but I'm still a wanted man."

"Well, at least you've got yourself a horse and a coat now. What're you doing back here?"

"Looking." Shannon pulled his tobacco sack out of a shirt pocket and offered it to the sheepherder.

"Thanks, but I like my pipe."

Tom rolled a smoke. "I think the man who killed Scott Wheeler is one of the wild bunch that's been making life dangerous for people in this part of the country. I'd like to find their hideout."

"I saw 'em. Three of 'em. Four days ago. They were on top of that hill there." The old man pointed north. "They disappeared over that hill." He yelled at one of his dogs and waved his right arm, and the dog went running and barking around the flank of the sheep herd and got it turned back south. The other dog kept its position on the opposite side of the herd, watching intently.

"You've got good help there." Tom grinned.

"They're smarter than most people and they work a hell of a lot harder."

"Well." Tom got back on his horse. "I'd sure like to find their camp, but"—he grinned a weak grin—"this time I hope to see them before they see me."

"Watch yourself."

At the top of the next hill, Shannon could look down into a long valley white with snow. He got off the crest where he wouldn't be so easy to spot, then stopped and studied the scene. It was then that the clouds parted and the sun came out. As desperate as he felt, Tom couldn't help but admire the beauty of the valley. Snow was piled on the tree limbs and covered the grass, and it was pure white without a blemish. The air was so clear it sparkled in the sunlight. Below him, a tall egg-shaped boulder stood on its end on a pile of smaller boulders and leaned against the green-timbered hillside.

But at the far end of the valley, about three miles away, the country was brown. Tom's eyes strained, trying to see what it was. He rode downhill, traversing the hill, and when he got closer he could see what it was. It was a dozen acres of scrub oak—buck brush—the kind that had saved his life back near Fortune. The brush was bare of leaves now.

Instead of riding to it, Tom turned his horse back uphill and climbed, stopping twice to let the animal blow. At the top he rode in the direction of the buck brush, but stayed out of sight of it. The sun was warming the air now and melting the snow.

It was late afternoon when he rode around the bottom of a hill and saw the buck brush again. This time he reined up sharply.

Tracks. Horse tracks. A shod horse.

"Uh-oh," Tom Shannon muttered. The tracks led right straight into the brush and they didn't come out. One horse could have been a cowboy making another search for cattle. Could have been one of the hardcases coming back from a night at Fortune.

One or the other.

He sat his horse, watching and thinking. What was on the other side? The country looked to be mostly low rolling hills to the east and high rocky hills to the north. Should he follow the tracks? No. Might ride right into their camp. Best way to see what was beyond the brush was to ride around it. He looked at the sky. The sun was close to the western horizon. Be dark in an hour. Have to travel.

Kicking the horse in the sides with spurless heels, Tom got it into a lope across a snow-covered park and into the hills. He was leaving tracks but he couldn't prevent it. On the upslopes he allowed the horse to walk, but he booted it into a lope on the downsides, knowing it might slip in the snow and fall, but knowing too that he had to hurry.

He rounded the bottom of a brush-covered hill and climbed another—and saw the horses.

A dozen—no, fifteen—horses were pawing the snow in a natural pocket back against a granite cliff. A rope was stretched across the pocket to keep the horses inside. Saddles lay on the ground near the rope.

Shannon got down and walked, leading his horse. The hair on the back of his neck came alive and a cold chill traveled up his spine. This was outlaw territory. He could be in someone's gunsights right now.

Near the top of the hill he stopped and dropped the reins, hoping the horse would stay put. Then, bent low, he walked to the top and looked down. They were there.

Tom dropped onto his stomach in the snow, took off his hat, and counted them. Seven. They had a three-sided shelter made of tree sections and a roof made of buck brush. Under it was a sheepherder's cookstove, a few pots and pans, and eight bedrolls.

The camp sat on a flat rocky acre surrounded by boulders and the buck brush. At first glance it appeared to be an easy target for men with rifles spotted on the hills. But after studying it, Tom could see that the boulders made an excellent fortress. At the first sign of danger, the men could get behind those rocks, and it would take cannon fire to rout them out. In fact, Tom guessed seven men could hold off an army there for hours. At least until dark. After dark they could get away. They could catch their horses and ride out in any direction, and they could be twenty miles away by daylight.

"Lord," he muttered.

He was tempted to go back to his horse, get his rifle, and put a bullet through that coffeepot down there just to see the men jump. But that would be foolish. No, the thing to do was get the hell out of there. Get out fast.

He backed away, crawling until he was out of sight of the camp, then stood up and ran to his horse. He gathered the reins and mounted. "Let's lope, old pony," he said.

Though he was riding in the dark again, Tom knew exactly where he was going, and he was traveling downhill, and he made better time than he did when he was searching. He kept the horse at a trot, and he guessed it was after midnight when he came to his burned-out cabin. By then the horse was so tired he had to whip it with the ends of the bridle reins at times to keep it going. He skirted the town of Fortune, and got back into the hills north of town and began trying to find his own camp. Trying to find it in the dark was useless, and he stopped, got down, loosened the cinch, and sat on a small boulder and waited for first light. The sorrel horse was glad to stop and rest. Shannon himself was so tired and sleepy he couldn't keep his eyes open, and he sat on the ground, leaned back against the boulder, and dozed, keeping his hold on the reins. At first light, he awakened, mounted, and located his camp.

There he unsaddled and picketed the horse and unrolled his tarp, blankets, and groceries. His growling stomach was constantly reminding him that he hadn't eaten since, Lord, how long? But he didn't build a fire. The sky was a clear blue and the air was still, and smoke could be seen for many miles. Instead he ate dried fruit and a can of tomatoes, and rolled up in his blankets and tarp and slept.

He awakened at noon, pulled on his boots, and looked around. The horse was lying down, flat on its side, and he walked over to it, hoping it was just resting and wasn't sick. The horse raised its head, threw its forefeet out in front, and got up.

"You're a good old pony," Tom said quietly. "I was lucky when I bought you. You're going to have a better time of it pretty soon. We're just about through with all this night riding. Just about, but not quite."

The snow was mostly gone from the open country, but back in the trees where the sun didn't shine the snow was still three inches deep.

Shannon ate more dried fruit, took a long drink out of the creek, and walked away from his camp. He walked two miles to where he could sit on the ground and see the town down on the plains four or five miles away. A freight wagon pulled by two horses was leaving town, going west on the Ute Trail road. Smoke from the sawmill's steam boiler rose almost straight up at the northeast corner of town. If men were looking for him, they were looking in the wrong direction.

Glancing at the sky, he wished daylight would end and darkness would come. He had to see Mary. They had to talk and make plans.

Tom knew now what he wanted to do, and he needed Mary's help.

CHAPTER 26

As usual she opened the back door in total darkness, and she wept a little with relief at finding him alive and unhurt. After she closed the heavy curtains and lit a lamp, she poured him a cup of coffee and remarked, "With that beard and a change of clothes, you could be mistaken for one of the old sourdoughs around here."

He grinned. "I've worn these clothes so long they could almost stand up by themselves."

"I've got a beef stew. I cooked it yesterday in hopes you'd come back last night. It will be ready to eat pretty soon." She lifted the lid on a black iron kettle, stirred the contents with a long-handled spoon, and sat. "What happened?"

"I found their hideout. I know where they are."

"You did?" Her eyes were wide. "How on earth did you find it?"

"Added things up. I told you about running into two of them up there, and I questioned V.C. Wheeler, and—"

She interrupted, "Wheeler? You questioned him?"

"Yeah. I went out to the Running W and questioned him the same way I questioned Tibalt—at the point of a gun. I was lucky enough to get away with it."

"You've been busy, haven't you?"

"Yeah. Old Wheeler didn't know anything that would help. Or at least he didn't tell me anything. Except that...he did say young Wheeler was prowling for cattle up there one day not long ago when he saw that faro dealer—what's his name? Henry Barrett?—and Barrett told him he was elk hunting."

Shannon paused and looked at Mary with a question in his eyes. "Tell me something. Does Barrett take his meals at the Silver Lode?"

"Yes, he does. He lives at the Fortune Hotel, you know."

"Uh-huh." Tom was speculative.

"Is that important, Tom?"

"Well, it—"

He was interrupted by a knocking on the front door. It was a polite knocking at first, then a loud hammering. A man's voice yelled, "Shannon. Tom Shannon. Come out of there. We know you're in there."

Tom didn't move. "Might as well take the stew off the stove, Mary. I sort of expected them. In fact, I want to meet with them. It was old Tibalt, no-doubt, who put them wise."

The hammering came again. "Shannon, we've got the doors and windows guarded. You can't get away. Open up."

Mary whispered, "What shall we do?"

"I want you out of here, Mary. Go to the front door and tell them you're coming out. Make sure they know it's you, then open the door and walk out."

"I can't do that. I can't just leave you to them."

"There's nothing else you can do. The only way you can help is let me use your house. They might get trigger happy, and I don't want you hurt."

"Is there no way out?"

"No. They're not bluffing. They know I'm in here and they think I might try to sneak out a window in the dark, and they've got all the windows guarded. Besides, I don't want out."

"Come out, Shannon. No use shooting. We don't want to hurt Mrs. Cress."

Tom struck a match and lit another lamp.

"What are you doing, Tom?"

"The only thing to do is invite them in. We've learned some things they ought to be interested in. Maybe they'll listen. I wish you were somewhere safe, though."

"I'm not leaving.''

He went through the house, lighting lamps. Then he yelled through the door, "I'm going to open the door. Come on in. There won't be any shooting."

Mary stood on a braided rug in the middle of the living room and wrung her hands.

When Tom unlatched and opened the door, three men poured in, guns drawn. There were C.H. Tibalt, Hugh March, owner of the Ore Bucket Hardware, and another man, a big, wide-shouldered bearded man whom Tom didn't recognize.

The big man said, "Evenin', Mary," then marched straight up to Tom and lifted his gun out of its holster. Hugh March went through the house and yelled, "Come on in, men. He's unarmed now."

Four more men came in through the front door.

Tom stood still, waiting, watching.

"I apologize, Mary," the big man said. He wore baggy denim pants with red suspenders. His thick-soled shoes were the lace-up kind. "I wish I didn't have to do this."

Among the four new arrivals were Zack Parmell and V.C. Wheeler. The other two were men Tom remembered seeing around town. Their faces were grim.

Mary said calmly, "Orville, won't you and these other gentlemen come into the kitchen and have some coffee?"

Hugh March answered. He was a medium-sized, middle-aged man with a bushy gray moustache. "Thanks, Mrs. Cress, but we've got some business to take care of here."

"And what would that be?" she asked.

"We've got to lock this feller up. He's been convicted of murder."

"And then what? Hang him?"

"Yes, ma'am. I'm sorry you got mixed up in this. You're a nice lady."

"He's been very busy," Mary said, looking March in the eye. "He's learned some things I'm sure you're interested in."

"Like what, Mrs. Cress?"

She waited for Tom to answer. Tom said simply, "I know where the killer gang is camped."

"You what?" It was, Tibalt asking.

"I found their hideout."

"You prob'ly knew where it was all along," March said.

Mary's voice was cold, terse. "No, he didn't. He's done more to try to find that gang than all of you put together."

"Why would you do that, Shannon?"

"Because," Tom spoke slowly, "I believe it was one of the gang that shot Scott Wheeler. And it was some of them that burned my cabin down."

"We—none of us—ever believed Shannon was part of the wild gang," Orville put in. "He's been convicted of murder, but we never thought he done anything else wrong."

"Aw," grumbled Tibalt, "putting the blame on that gang, that's too easy. Of course he'd say that."

Wheeler snapped, "Shannon, have you any evidence to back that up?"

"Some."

"Spill it then."

"Why don't you gentlemen come into the kitchen," Mary said. "I'll put the coffee on. You can talk in there."

"Thank you just the same, Mrs. Cress," repeated Hugh March, "but we didn't come here to drink coffee."

"If he knows something about that gang, I'll listen to him," Zack Parmell said. "But I'm keeping a gun on him."

"That's all we ask." Mary went into the kitchen, and Tom followed, careful not to make any quick moves. Parmell and Orville were right behind him, six-guns ready. Wheeler hesitated, then went in too. Soon they were all in the kitchen. "I don't have enough chairs," Mary said. "I hope some of you don't mind sitting on the floor."

Tom dropped onto the floor and sat with his back against a wall. Orville sat next to him, a gun in his hand. Parmell sat cross-legged six feet away. The others occupied chairs around the kitchen table. Mary busied herself putting more wood in the stove. She put a galvanized coffeepot on top. Everyone was looking at Shannon.

"All right," he said, "there had to be a reason someone shot Scott Wheeler. I mean, other than meanness or revenge. It wasn't me, so it had to be someone with a reason."

"You had a reason," March said.

"Besides," Wheeler, said, "we're not here to conduct a trial. Whatever you've got to say about my son's murder can be said in a court of law."

"He's already been tried," said Hugh March.

Mary was sitting at the table with her hands folded. "I was hoping you gentlemen would be interested in finding the outlaw gang and doing something about that. Tom knows where they are."

"Yeah, you did say something about that, Shannon." Zack Parmell was staring at him as if trying to look inside him.

"I found their hideout. But..." Tom paused, swallowed, "it would take an army to surround them, and if there was any shooting they'd get more of us then we'd get of them."

"Where is it?"

"Up there." Tom nodded toward the high country. "East and north. It would be hard to tell you. I can lead you there. But like I said, it would cost the lives of too many good men."

"I'm so damned sick of that bunch I'll lead the attack myself," said C.H. Tibalt.

"We have to get them at all costs," said Wheeler. "We can count on every man that works for the Running W," said Zack Parmell. "We can round up whatever number of men and guns it takes."

"I can get half a dozen from the sawmill," Orville said. "They've had their payroll stole so many times they'd be tickled to get shot at if they got a chance to shoot back."

Tom shook his head sadly. "Sure, if you rounded up enough men with guns, you'd get some of them. But not all. Some would get away. And their guns would take a heavy toll."

"Maybe it would be worth it," Tibalt said.

"There's got to be a better way," Tom said, still shaking his head.

"What?" Parmell asked. "Have you got an idea?"

"Well, uh, I was thinking. Maybe what we ought to do is..." He paused, trying to think of the way to say it, wondering whether the plan he had in mind would work. Seven men were waiting for him to continue.

Mary broke the quiet. "I think the coffee's ready." She stood, took china cups from a wooden cupboard, and poured coffee. "I've got sugar but no cream. Anyone want sugar?"

No one did, and she served the coffee black and unsweetened.

Each man took a cup and sipped. Tom sipped his coffee, blew on it to cool it off, and took another sip. He set the cup on the floor between his knees

"We might set a trap for them."

Parmell set his cup on the floor too. "How?"

Shannon looked around the room at the men facing him. They were listening. "I've been thinking about it and maybe it will work. But"—again his eyes met every eye in the room—"it means secrecy. If the word got out it wouldn't work. You all have to be sure of who you're talking to about it. The gang has men in town. In fact, I believe they're everywhere."

Silence. The men sipped their coffee.

Wheeler grunted, shifted in his chair, and said, "Well, we've suspected for some time now that they have eyes and ears in the right places. We don't know whose eyes and ears, but they seem to know everything. It would be difficult to keep a secret from them."

"What's your plan, Shannon?"

"Well..." Again he wasn't sure the men would agree with him. But he had to try. "The best place to trap them would be out in an open spot where we have plenty of cover. But I don't know how to do that. So I was thinking maybe the next best place would be here in town."

"Uh-huh," Wheeler grunted. "How would you get them here?"

"Make them think there's something here that's worth stealing. Make them think it will take the whole gang to steal it."

"What would that be?"

"Well, I..." Tom had to look down. "I haven't figured that out. I was hoping one of you would have an idea."

"Surely you can think of something," Mary said.

"Aw, wait a minute now." Hugh March was scowling. "Wait just a doggone minute. We came here to arrest an escaped killer. What are we doing? We're sitting around drinking coffee and talking to him like he was one of us and listening to him try to worm his way out."

Mary snapped at him, "He is one of you. He's no killer. He wants to rid this county of that gang and he wants to clear his name. Can't you listen to him?"

"Well, then." V.C. Wheeler was the wealthiest man among them and he commanded respect. "Tom Shannon was convicted of killing my only offspring. Nobody on God's earth wants my son's killer hung more than I do. But I'm willing to give Shannon another trial. Maybe the first one was too quick."

"It was a real honest-to-God trial," said March.

"It wasn't foolproof," Wheeler answered. "No, I'm not saying he's innocent. He's got to prove that to me. But if he helps us stomp out a gang of cutthroats that has been robbing and murdering folks in Park County for the past eight months, then I'm for giving him another chance, another trial."

"Can you prove you didn't do it, Shannon?" It was Parmell asking.

"I don't know. I've got a hunch. Well, more than just a hunch. But no real proof. I need some time and I need to ask more questions. I can't ask questions in a jail cell."

"You don't think we're going to just turn you loose, do you?" March asked.

Tom lifted his hands and let them fall in a hopeless gesture.

Orville stood up and poured himself another cup of coffee. "Mighty good java, Mary. Did I hear right? Did I hear you bought a house and lot in his name?"

"Yes."

"Why'd you do that?"

"Because he's innocent and I believe he will prove it. When he does, he'll need a house." Her voice turned sour. "Somebody...some mean, sneaky, poor excuse for a man burned down his cabin, you know."

"If I knew who done it, I'd be after him," Orville said. "That's just as bad as stealin'. It's worse than stealin'. Burnin' down a man's home like that."

"I'm convinced," Tom said, "that everyone here in this room would do anything to get rid of that killer bunch. You all would risk your lives. There's got to be a way."

151

C.H. Tibalt spoke up, "We can't make them think there's money in the bank, because there's no bank."

"They ran the bank out of town."

"What else would bring them to town?"

"Use your imaginations," Mary said. "Think of something big enough to attract the whole gang."

"Money. Or gold."

"Well then, now," Wheeler said, "where would it come from and where would it be stashed?"

"And why would it be stashed in Fortune?"

Silence. Mary stood and put more wood in the stove. She sat with her elbows on the table and her chin in her hands.

"If it came on the stage it would go right out on the stage."

"Unless it was brought here to finance something. What could it be?"

"They know about every money or gold shipment that comes through here."

"But maybe the bank in Fairplay could get wise and try to sneak some money past them."

"That's an idea," Mary said. "Wagons carrying little of value come through here all the time. People moving. Prospectors and their families giving up and going east. They carry nothing but their personal belongings."

"Yeah. If I was trying to sneak some money through Fortune, that's the way I'd do it."

"Sure," Mary continued. "Disguise some men to look like a man and woman who have nothing worth stealing and are driving a team and wagon from Fairplay to the east someplace."

"Hmmm."

"And you could put out the word that the wagon is full of money, but broke an axle and is going to be in Fortune until it's fixed and the couple is on their way."

"That'd fetch 'em," Orville grinned.

"Might work," said Wheeler.

"The beauty of it is, we don't really need a fake couple or even a busted-up wagon. Just make them think we have."

"Let the word slip out. They'll hear it."

Tom re-crossed his ankles and put in, "We have to have some timing here. We not only have to bring them to town, we have to know when they're coming."

"Yeah. If we knew when and where, we could sure make it mighty uncomfortable for 'em."

"We've got to do better than that. We've got to wipe them out."

Mary was getting excited and the lift in her voice showed it. "Now you're talking. You'll think of a way."

"Yeah, let's get down to the details now."

"Now then," Wheeler said, "what we've got—supposedly got— is two men disguised as a man and woman bringing a load of money through Fortune. They busted an axle or a wheel on their wagon and they're stuck here until they get it fixed. They've got a trunk full of money of some kind. Where would they put it while they're waiting for their wagon to be fixed?"

"In the jail. That would be the safest place. There's nobody in it now, and it can be locked up. If I had to leave some money in town, that's where I'd put it."

"Right you are. We could put an empty trunk in there and a guard at the door, and everybody but us would believe there was a lot of money in that trunk."

"Now you're thinking," Mary said, excited.

"But," Tom cautioned, "you've got a lot of planning to do. This has to be done with a lot of thinking and planning."

"Right you are. We can't just run off half-cocked."

"We've got to be ready for them."

"Ooh." Mary suddenly lost her enthusiasm. "My gosh. It means a lot of shooting, doesn't it. Someone will be killed."

"If we do it right, only the wild bunch will be killed," said Wheeler. "We can take cover while they'll be in the open. They'll be in the street."

"The children. What about the women and children?" Mary asked.

"We'll have to get them out of the way. In their houses on the floor."

"And that," said Tom, shaking his head again, "won't be easy."

"Why?"

"Because it means telling almost everyone in town to take cover. The gang will hear about it."

"Aw, damn. Excuse me, Mrs. Cress, I mean darn."

Silence. Coffee cups were cold by now and the coffeepot was empty. Then Wheeler spoke up. "We have to try. Maybe it won't work. They might get wise to us. But we have to try."

Several men nodded in agreement.

"We'll have to get the message to the women to keep their kids in their houses, and do it without sending a message to the gang."

"It's all we can do."

"Be mighty careful who you talk to about this."

Zack Parmell stood and stretched. "We've sat here in Mrs. Cress's kitchen and talked most of the night away. I've got work to do at the ranch. What say we meet again tomorrow night and talk this over some more."

"You can't wait," Tom said. "Their camp isn't the kind of place where a bunch of men want to spend the winter. They'll be moving on."

"That'd be one way of getting rid of 'em."

"But they'd be back. Park County has been easy pickin's. If they don't come back, another bunch just like them will. We've got to wipe them out and let the whole wide world know about it."

"We can't let them get away."

"Tomorrow night, then. Tomorrow night we make some tight plans. But keep quiet about this. Be damned quiet. Excuse me, Mrs. Cress, be danged quiet."

"What about Shannon here? Are we going to just let him go?"

"We can't do that."

"Then what?"

They were silent as they mulled it over. Zack Parmell broke the silence with a chuckle. "We can't put him in jail with all that money, can we?"

Others chuckled with him. Then C.H. Tibalt turned serious. "Mary, I've known you ever since you and your husband came here, and I knew you when your husband was killed. My wife was one of the women who sat with you that night and all the next day and the next night. She said you are one of the most honest women she ever met. Will you give us your word that Tom Shannon will be here tomorrow night?"

She answered quickly and simply, "Yes."

"That's good enough for me," said Wheeler.

"Remember, don't tell anyone. And leave your horses someplace else and walk over here. Don't do anything suspicious."

They left.

The next thing Shannon did was take care of his horse. He pumped a bucket of water and took it out, then checked the fence around Mary's back yard and off-saddled the animal. "Good thing you didn't cut the grass in your backyard," he said when he went back inside. "There's enough there to feed a horse three or four days." He grinned. "I'll have to do some manure shoveling when this is over."

"Do you think it will be over soon, Tom?"

"Yeah. One way or another, it's coming to an end." He grinned again. "I'm as hungry as a pet bear. Put that stew back on the stove, will you?"

CHAPTER 27

Tom Shannon was restless. Though he no longer was hiding in the dark, he was confined to Mary's house. "It wouldn't do to go out on the streets and be recognized," he said. "Someone would recognize me and wonder what the heck is going on."

"Can't spill the beans," Mary said. She fixed Tom's breakfast of pancakes and sausage, then left for her job at the Silver Lode.

Tom prowled through the house. He wondered what the neighbors would think when they saw a horse grazing in Mary's backyard. She had no stable to put the horse in. He wondered what kind of house and lot Mary had bought in his name. It had a stable, she had said. Like to see it, he thought. But...aw, hell. More important things to do.

He picked up some of Mary's books and looked through them. There were four copies of Shakespeare's plays, two books by Charles Dickens and there was a book titled *Dr. Stowe's Home Medicine Book*. Still another was titled *How To Get Rich In Real Estate*.

He looked out the window at his horse. The animal had eaten its fill and was standing in a corner of the lot with its eyes half-closed, sleeping on its feet. Tom wondered what kind of muscles kept a horse's knees from buckling while it slept standing up, and he wished he had the same ability.

I owe you, old horse, he thought. Where would mankind be without the beasts of burden?

The day was partly cloudy outside, with strong, gusty winds, but the bitter cold of winter hadn't arrived yet. The snow that had fallen was gone now. There would be more. A lot more.

Dark came early that time of year, and the Silver Lode stayed open until long after dark. Shannon closed the curtains and lit a lamp. He warmed up the stew and found it was even better than it had been the night before. It had had time to jell, as the sheepherder would say.

When finally Mary came home, Orville was with her. The three of them waited in the kitchen. Within an hour the five townsmen and the owner and foreman of the Running W Ranch were gathered there, sipping hot black coffee. Tom hoped someone else would act as chairman of the meeting, but no one offered to.

"I think we've got as good a plan as we can figure out," he said. "Have you all decided who you can trust to take part in it?"

"I've got two good men lined up," Orville said "They're two I know I can trust."

"I'll bring four from the Running W," Wheeler said. "With me and Zack, that'll make six of us."

"Added to us here, that'll make, uh, fourteen,"

Tom said. "Just to be sure, we could use a few more."

"How many of them do you think there are, Tom?"

"I counted eight bedrolls, so there'll be that many. We need to outnumber them two to one or better. Maybe, when they see how they're outnumbered, maybe they'll give up with no one getting hurt."

"I've got a neighbor who's been robbed and knocked in the head by that gang," said C.H. Tibalt. "We can count on him."

Mary said, "My boss, Mr. Brown, would like to get in on this. He has complained bitterly about how terrible business is now that the gang has caused so many people to leave town."

Tom shook his head. "He'd have to close the cafe, and that might look suspicious."

"We don't want anything suspicious," said Parmell. "We have to have everything looking normal. Not too many horses on the streets."

"But enough," added Hugh March. "If there aren't any horses or people on the streets, that'd look suspicious."

"That's going to be one of our biggest problems," Shannon said. "Some innocent people might get hit."

"And the worst of it is, we don't know for sure who is a member of that gang and who isn't."

"The way I see it," said Tibalt, "is we're all taking a chance on getting killed. It's the only way. I wish to God there was another way, but there isn't."

"People on the street will just have to take their chances too."

"But not the children," Mary put in.

"Right. We've got to get the word to the women to keep their kids at home."

"There ain't too many women and kids left in Fortune," said Orville.

"No, that's right, but we've got to protect what few there are."

"Mary"—Tom was looking at her with a worry furrow between his eyes—"can you do it?"

"Yes. I know most of the women. I'll tell them. And I'll be sure to tell them the importance of keeping it quiet."

"All right," Tom said, "we know what we're going to do. Try to find a few more men you know you can trust. We'll have to have sharpshooters, two or more, at each end of the block so no one can get out of town that way, and we'll have to cover the alley behind the jail, two good men there. The roofs may be the best places. We'll put two or three across the street in Mr. Tibalt's store. They can fortify the windows. The rest of us will have to find positions where we can shoot without making good targets of ourselves."

"You were in the war," Tibalt said, "and you were a leader. Suppose you tell us which positions to take. Somebody has to decide, otherwise we'd have too many men in one spot and not enough in another."

"Mr. Wheeler ranked higher in the army than I did. He'd make a fine battlefield commander."

"No," said Wheeler. "I didn't dodge nearly as much lead as you and Zack. As far as I'm concerned, you're in charge, Tom."

"I'd just as soon someone else took charge. How about you, Zack?"

"Nope," Parmell answered. "Whatever you say, I'll do it."

"Say"—March squinted at Tom—"you aren't going to take advantage of all the gunfire and confusion and run again, are you?"

Mary exploded, "That's preposterous. He escaped once and got all the way to Tarryall. You're not so dumb as to think he came back just so he could have the fun of escaping again, are you?"

"Tom's the boss. At least for this job." Orville's jaw was set inside the bushy beard.

"Keep in mind one thing, Shannon." Wheeler's thick gray eyebrows came together. "You're still a convicted murderer. I'm willing to go along with this because I want to get rid of that gang of killers and thieves and I'll do anything to bring that about. Yeah, I'll even take orders from you."

"Is that a promise? From all of you?" Tom looked each man in the eye. One by one, they all nodded in agreement.

Mary spoke calmly. "Looks like you're elected, Tom."

"All right. Mary, we have to depend on you. You tell the women to keep off the street and keep their kids in the house day after tomorrow. And tomorrow, you let it be known, in the usual cafe conversation, that a wagon carrying a trunk full of money broke down just west of town and the money is being kept in the jail."

"Zack, you mention it to the bartender at the Salty Dog and anyone else who might be within hearing distance. Make sure several men hear it, but don't make a big show of it."

"Mr. Tibalt, you do the same in your store. Say the wagon will be fixed day after tomorrow and the money will be on its way."

"And..." Tom stopped talking. Suddenly his face was screwed up in worry. "I just thought of something. If they thought the wagon would be on its way in a couple of days, they'd wait until it was out of town and then attack."

"Oh-oh," said Parmell. "We've got a problem there."

"We'll have to lie some more," said Orville. "Say an army of special guards is expected in a couple of days to escort the wagon to Tarryall and beyond."

"Yeah. They'd figure the best place to steal it is right here in town. Before the guards get here."

"I'd bet a dollar," March said, "they'll plan to make this their last big robbery before winter, then clear out till spring."

"And then they'd come right back and raise hell with us again."

"I think you've got the right idea, Orville," Tom said. "That's the story we'll—you'll—put out. I'll have to keep out of sight until you see them coming. We don't want anyone curious about me walking around free."

"We've got a wagon at the ranch, and one of my men is a little man. We can start out early in the morning, circle the town, and come in from the west with two of my men in the wagon. Shorty can put on some of my late wife's clothes. I can even find a steamer trunk."

"Fine," Tom said, "Can you time it so you get to town about midmorning?"

"We can time it any way you want."

"That's what we'll do then. Zack, you get on top of the bank building day after tomorrow and watch for them. That's the tallest building in town, and from there you can see for miles to the east. You'll give us a signal when you see them coming, and we'll take our places."

"I'll do 'er."

"Are you going to decide who takes what place, Tom?"

"Yeah. Someone has to do that. I'll go out on the street at first light in the morning, before the town gets out of bed, and try to figure out where the best spots are."

"Are we all set then?" Wheeler asked.

"One more thing," Shannon said. "In all the robberies they've pulled, they wore black rags around their faces. That'll make them easy to pick out when the shooting first starts. But once the shooting starts, they'll probably throw away those masks and try to look like honest citizens. No doubt some of them are men you'll recognize. We have to be careful. We can't let them get away, and we don't want to shoot any innocent people either."

"It ought to be a short battle," Parnell said. "We ought to pick them off before they realize what's happening."

"Does that mean, then, that we're not taking any prisoners?" Wheeler's face was grim. "Personally, I don't condone so much bloodshed if it can be avoided."

"If it can be avoided, neither do I," Tom answered. "But unless they throw up their hands in the middle of the street, we have no choice but to shoot."

"They never gave nobody a fightin' chance," Orville said.

"I thought I was through with war. But I don't see any other way."

"It's war, all right," Parmell said. "That's exactly what it is. It's us or them."

Outside the autumn wind moaned around the eaves of the house. A lamp flickered and went out, its wick dry. Two other lamps illuminated the faces of the men. They were not happy faces. But each face had a hard, determined set to it.

Shannon spoke quietly, "Anyone want to back out? Any second thoughts?"

No one moved.

"That's it, then. Keep your rifles handy but not where they can be seen. Don't be too loud when you're passing out false information, but be sure the word gets around."

"Our wagon will be here by ten-thirty in the morning," Wheeler said. "We'll pull a wheel off right out by the bank building where everyone will see it, and we'll carry the trunk into the jail."

Still no one moved until Zack Parmell stood and chuckled. "I'll tell Shorty to shave off his whiskers. But even with a fresh shave, he's got a face no woman would want."

Orville chuckled too. "I know old Shorty. He's gonna be the ugliest woman I ever saw."

A ripple of chuckles swept through the room. Then died.

"When they come—if they come—it'll probably be before noon," Tom said. "If it happens, it'll be over by noon day after tomorrow."

"If it doesn't happen, well..." Wheeler shrugged. "We tried."

"If it doesn't happen, it will be because they were warned or because they've already left this part of the country."

"As much as I hate killing, I hope it happens."

They all stood.

"Thanks for the java, Mary."

"Thanks for letting us use your house, Mrs. Cress."

"Tom"—Wheeler stood in front of him—"I hope you can prove you didn't kill my son."

"If you want the guilty man, Mr. Wheeler, just aim true. I'd bet—in fact I know—that one of those men we'll be firing at is the man who shot Scott Wheeler."

"I hope you can prove that."

"I hope so too, Mr. Wheeler."

They filed out in the dark.

Mary dropped wearily into a kitchen chair, put her elbows on the table and her face in her hands. "Are we doing the right thing, Tom?" She looked up at him, agony in her face. "Do we have to have all this killing?"

"Yeah." He sat opposite her. "It's like Zack Parmell said, it's them or us. It's war. It really is."

CHAPTER 28

They talked until another lamp burned low, flickered, and went out. Mary went into a small room that held no furniture and was used as a storage room. She came back carrying a gallon can of coal oil. Shannon took it from her and refilled the two lamps, lit one of them.

He ran his fingers over his beard and said, "Wish I had my razor. I'd cut off this tangle of brush. If I don't, some pack rat's going to build a nest in it."

"I've got one. My late husband's. You'll have to sharpen it, but I've got a razor strop too."

"Good. I'll put some water on the stove." He pumped a tea kettle full of water, put it on the stove, and stoked the fire. "What would your late husband think if he knew another man was using his razor, sleeping in his house, sleeping in his bed, and—"

She cut him off. "If he knew you, he'd be happy about it."

"I'm not so sure he'd be happy about me, but he couldn't expect a pretty young woman like you to stay alone the rest of your life."

"No, he wouldn't expect that."

When the tea kettle whistled, he poured the water into a shallow pan, propped a small mirror on the windowsill over the kitchen sink, and picked up the razor and leather strop she had brought him. He whetted the razor with a practiced hand, lathered his face with soap, grimaced at his reflection in the mirror, and said, "Well, old feller, in a few minutes you're going to look like a peeled onion."

She laughed when he finished. "You look funny, Tom. You're

163

spotted."

"Spotted? How?"

"Your face is two shades of color. No, three."

He looked at himself again in the mirror and laughed with her.

"Look at you. Your forehead that's been covered by a hat is one shade of white, your nose and your face from the eyebrows down to your cheeks is brown from the sun, and your cheeks and chin are lady white."

"Yeah," he chuckled, "and if I ever get a haircut, that'll leave some more white spots. I'm going to have to get out in the sun with my hat off to get some color back."

"If you don't, children will be pointing at you."

He was out of bed and dressed before daylight. She was right behind him in her long nightgown, wiping sleep from her eyes with her fingertips. "I'll put the coffee on," she said. "You can eat breakfast when you get back."

"You'll have to go to work before I get back. I'll fix my own breakfast."

"Yes. The Silver Lode has to feed the early shift at the sawmill."

At the first sign of light he went out onto the street. The town was quiet except for a dog barking somewhere. He shivered in the cold and shoved his hands deep into his jacket pockets. It was three blocks to the jail and he got there without being seen. At the jail, he stopped and looked around. Tibalt's wood-frame mercantile was across the street from the jail and it had a window on each side of the door. That was good. Men with rifles could barricade themselves behind those windows.

Next to the mercantile was a vacant building, once a rooming house. The windows and doors were boarded up. A long plank fence ran between it and the Ore Bucket Hardware on the corner. Be hard to climb over that fence.

So that side of the street should be easy to defend. No escape there. But the other side wasn't so good. There was that weed-grown lot next to the jail—where the gallows stood. A full moon hung low in the eastern sky, casting a gray shadow on the west side of the building. But not on the gallows. The gallows platform and headframe were above the shadows, standing there, menacing, waiting for a victim. Tom couldn't keep a shiver from running through his body at the sight of the gallows. He had to force his eyes away from it.

The lot would be a handy escape route for the gang. East of it was a laundry, and on the other side of the laundry was the vacant bank building. On the other side of the jail was an assay office.

All right, Tom thought, the doors to all the buildings could be locked just before the shooting starts. That left the vacant lot and the street as the only escape routes.

Shannon walked between the buildings, through the weed-grown lot, past the gallows to an alley. Two men with rifles could stand behind the buildings in the alley and shoot around the corners at anyone, who tried to run through the vacant lot. Be better if one of the two is left-handed. Have to ask about that.

Those two will be busy. Have to have good repeating rifles. If one or two of them is hit, the gang will pour through that lot like a bunch of rats through a hole in a barn. Need more than two men. Need some fortifications. Well, they can always dig a hole. All right, dig a hole in the ground and put one or two men in it. Four men could cut off that escape route. That'd drive the gang back to the street. Now, got to cut off escape that way.

Shannon stood in the middle of the street. He tried to picture in his mind what would happen. Let's see. First, they'll leave a couple of men in the street to hold the horses. Five or six will go into the deputy's office and the jail. Can't let them take over in there. If they did, they could shoot out the window. Got to have at least four men inside there, barricaded some way. When the gang sees they can't get in the jail, they'll back out into the street and try to get to their horses. That's when the men across the street in Tibalt's store will open up. The battle should be over very soon after that.

But suppose it isn't?

All right, they'll try to get through that vacant lot or they'll try to go down the street. When they run into gunfire from the vacant lot they'll head down the street. Can't be many of them left by then. But they might get lucky.

Need some sharpshooters at each end of the block. Got to keep the battle in one block. Less chance of getting innocent civilians hit that way. Civilians? Shannon smiled a grim smile. We're all civilians. This is no military battle.

Let's see. Four men in the jail. Four men guarding the vacant lot. That's eight. Two or more in Tibalt's store. That's ten. Really ought to have more in the store. Say four. That'd be twelve. Need at least two at each end of the block. On the roofs or shooting around corners. March's hardware store is at the west end of the block and it has a false front. Good place for a rifleman. On the roof behind that false front. Now about the other end of the block. Their camp is east and north. They'll try to head east. Let's see.

The vacant bank building. Made of native stone. Good spot. Men could shoot out the windows.

That's it, then. How many men we put in Tibalt's store and in the jail depends on how many men we have. Tom took a long last look around. It ought to work. If it works right, they'll see there's no escape and they'll drop their guns and throw up their hands. If it works right, there won't be so much gunfire.

Bright daylight was coming fast. Shannon had to get off the street. Looks good, he said to himself. But he knew from experience that the best plans often go wrong. Except for Zack Parmell and V.C. Wheeler, his troops—the men on his side—had never been in battle. The hardcases were experienced gunfighters.

There was no way to predict what would happen.

Back at Mary's house, he found she had gone to work. A penciled note in a neat hand was on the kitchen table beside a crock of pancake batter. It said Mary would get the message to the women in town even if she had to knock on their doors during the afternoon lull in the cafe business, and it advised Tom to make himself hard to see.

He poured pancake batter onto a flat frying pan and cooked his meal. Then it was restless time again.

He tried to read some of Mary's books but couldn't concentrate. In his mind he could see men shooting, men falling, horses falling, dead bodies, dying men. A terrible cold feeling of uncertainty swept through him, chilled him. Had he made a mistake? Men would die because of his plan. And what if it didn't work? What if the wild bunch had already quit the country, or what if they were warned off? He would be sneered at. No one would ever take him seriously again.

Worse, he would still be a convicted killer waiting for a hangman's noose. The townsmen would be so disgusted with him, there would be no second trial. If his plan didn't work he would be running again. Running and hiding in the dark. Without Mary.

No, by God, he thought, I'm not running anymore. Not ever again.

It was midafternoon when Mary came home. He was full of questions. Did the wagon get to town? Yes, she said. There were people in it, a man and what looked to be a woman in a sunbonnet. Mary smiled a wry smile. The sunbonnet was out of place that time of year. She hoped no one would notice that. The wagon was pulled by two horses and it looked for all the world like a wagon carrying the worldly possessions of a man and his wife traveling across country.

They even had some chairs and a bedstead in it. Mary had seen the wagon stop in front of the bank building, and the man and fake woman had carried a trunk down the street and into the jail. She had seen two more men from the blacksmith shop across the alley pull the rear wheels off the wagon and leave it with the rear end propped up in the street. The team had been unhitched and led away.

"I saw a man come out of the Salty Dog and into the cafe, and I told him I'd heard rumors about that wagon. He was interested. I told him. I'd heard from a man in business clothes that a wagon was carrying a lot of money from the bank at Fairplay. He wanted to know more, but I pretended I didn't know any more, and I suddenly got very busy."

"Looks like everything is going the way we planned it."

"So far. Well, I've got to go, Tom. There are two women I haven't seen yet. And I have to get back to work soon. Can you, uh, can you fix your own supper? I won't get back until nine o'clock."

He grinned crookedly. "Sure. I've been a bachelor a long time."

She stood on tiptoe and kissed him on the mouth. "You may not know it, Mr. Tom Shannon, but your bachelor days are numbered."

Grinning, he said, "I've been thinking about that when I wasn't thinking about how to stay alive."

A worry frown crossed her face. "It's exciting, what's about to happen, but it's worrisome too."

His smile vanished. "Yeah. I wish it was someone else's idea and not mine. I wish someone else had taken charge."

"You know, Tom..." She had her arms around his neck, but she leaned back, her wide gray eyes locked onto his. "The main problem in Fortune is the lack of leadership. Ever since Deputy Atwell was killed, no one has been willing to take charge of anything. I've always believed that with the right kind of leadership this town would not only survive, but prosper. It has all the natural resources and everything else a town needs. Except leadership. You're a leader, Tom. You're what this town needs."

Shaking his head, he said, "I hope you'll still believe that this time tomorrow."

"No matter what happens, I'll always believe in you." She kissed him again and left.

CHAPTER 29

He prowled through the house, sat, paced back and forth, smoked, drank coffee, smoked. He wanted to go out onto the streets, see what was happening. He didn't dare. Someone would recognize him and say to someone else, "What is Tom Shannon doing walking around free? Why ain't he locked up? Or dead? What's going on around here?"

Tom smoked, paced, smoked.

For supper he opened a can of corn and warmed it on the stove. That and some fried bacon and cold bread was all he wanted. He didn't really want that. He had to force himself to eat. Going hungry wouldn't accomplish anything. He had no more than finished eating and stacking the dirty dishes in a wash pan when he heard the first knock on the front door.

It was Orville and two men from the sawmill.

Tom put the coffeepot on and answered another knock on the door. This time it was C.H. Tibalt and a neighbor he introduced as Harry Toombs. Within an hour there were thirteen men in the room—fourteen, counting Tom.

He poured coffee in Mary's china mugs, passed them around, and sat on the floor. "Is this all?" he asked.

"Yeah," said Tibalt. "I know that ninety-five percent of the men in this town are honest, God-fearing citizens, but there's that other five percent. And I don't know for sure who they are."

"There are others I know," March said, "but some of them,

while they're honest, have a way of talking too much."

"I brought every man from the ranch that I know I can count on," said Wheeler. "There are a couple of others, but I'm not sure what they'd do in a battle."

"I'm like Mr. Tibalt," Orville put in. "I know nearly ever'body at the sawmill is honest. But that wild bunch knows exactly when there's money in the safe, and I don't know who tells 'em."

"I'd like to have more guns," Shannon said, "but it's better to have a handful of men we know we can depend on than a hundred who might do the wrong thing."

"The wrong kind of men could wreck our plan," said Tibalt. "And shoot each other."

"Have you got the plan, I mean, all the details, worked out, Tom?"

"Yeah. I took a good look at the street this morning. It's not perfect, but it's not too bad either. Here's the way I see it..."

He explained it in detail and assigned each man a position, then asked, "Is anyone left-handed?"

"Old Bert is," Orville answered. "Ain't you, Bert?"

"Yeah," said the sawyer from the sawmill. "I've got one of them repeatin' rifles that throws the empties out to one side and I'm always gettin hit in the face with 'em." He added with a grin, "It don't hurt, howsomever."

"Fine. Then, you and Orville take places in the alley where you can shoot around a corner without exposing too much of yourselves."

"We got some attention when we carried that trunk inside the jail," said the cowboy called Shorty. "One feller even asked what was in it. I didn't answer 'cuz I can't talk like a woman, but Zeke told 'im it's a secret. You shoulda seen that feller's eyes bug out."

"I'm bettin' he hot-footed it to the Salty Dog and spread the word that somethin' valuable's locked up in the jail."

"He sure did," said Zack Parmell. "I heard him. I told him— loud enough that some of the others could hear—that I'd heard a squad of soldiers was coming day after tomorrow to help move it somewhere east."

"The word's been spread. A regular customer of mine came into the store and ask me if I'd heard about it. I said I had. I winked at him and said it was just a rumor, though, and I didn't know if it was true."

Orville grinned inside his bushy beard. "That'll fetch 'em."

"Have you all got good guns? Rifles?"

Every man nodded.

"All right, Zack, you get on the roof of the bank building early in the morning. You might have a long wait, but it's better to be early than late. When you see them coming, climb down and pass the word along the block. Orville, you and your pals make sure every door in that block is locked, then take your positions."

"Wheeler, turn one of those steel cots over inside the deputy's office, and you and your men get behind it. Don't shoot until they try to come in the door, and be careful who you shoot at. You were an army commander, Wheeler. You know how to control your men. Give them a chance to surrender, but if they don't, shoot."

"The rest of you, when you hear shooting from the jail, get those rifles to your shoulders and take aim. Take good aim. Don't hit innocent people. If they throw up their hands, don't shoot them, but keep them in your sights."

While they were talking, Mary came home. Every man stood and greeted her with words like, "Evenin', Mrs. Cress." "Welcome to your own home, Mrs. Cress." She took off her heavy wool sweater and dropped wearily into a kitchen chair that Zack Parmell vacated for her.

"I've talked to all the women with children," she said. "They were surprised and curious. I warned them to keep it to themselves. I told them not to mention to anyone that something was going to happen. I didn't tell them what was going to happen, only that something might happen and they should keep their kids in the house. I hope they heed my warning."

"You done the best you could, Mary," Orville said.

"Where are you going to be, Shannon?" asked Hugh March.

"I'm going to be in the bank building. I can stay out of sight there until I'm needed, and I'll have a good view of the street from there. If they pour too much lead at Orville and his two partners, I can run around back of the bank building and help out."

"It looks," said V.C. Wheeler, "that the hottest spots will be the vacant lot and the east end of the block where the bank building is."

"That's the way I see it too. Orville, if you can recruit some more help, you ought to do it."

"We'll hold 'em," Orville said, looking at his two co-workers from the sawmill. They nodded in agreement.

"Would you gentlemen like some more coffee?" asked Mary.

"No thank you, Mrs. Cress." Wheeler stood and stretched. "We've talked enough. We've done everything we can to make this plan work. If it doesn't work, nobody will be to blame."

"It'll work."

"If it doesn't, if they don't come, we've tried."

"I only hope," Mary said, "that none of you get hurt. I'm going to pray for you."

They all stood. "I'd appreciate that, Mrs. Cress."

"There's nothing more to say. We all know what to do. Let's get some sleep, and when the time comes, do it."

When they were alone, Mary sat at the table with her chin in her hands. "I don't think I'll sleep much, Tom. I'm going to lie awake all night worrying."

"Try to get some sleep, Mary. Maybe nothing will happen."

She sighed, stood, and started unbuttoning her dress. "Either nothing will happen, or...as my late husband would say, all hell is going to bust loose."

CHAPTER 30

They were up before daylight, eating a hastily cooked breakfast. When they parted, she kissed him long and hard and held him tight for several long moments before she let him go. "God bless you, darling."

He carried the rifle and six-gun he had taken from the deputy's office as he walked to the vacant bank building. It was breaking daylight when he got there. With his bare hands he pried a board loose from a front window, then used the rifle butt to break the glass. He had to get inside off the street without being seen.

A chilly wind was whistling down from the north, but the sky was clear.

His footsteps sounded hollow on the wooden floor of the empty building. The wrought iron tellers' cages and the long pine barrister that separated the public section of the long room from the offices were all still there. The desks were gone and so was the big iron safe that had once stood against the far wall. Everything was covered with a layer of dust.

Shannon shook his head sadly when he remembered how easy it had been for the gang to blast open that safe. They had killed a guard one night. One held a gun on him and another came up behind him and cut his throat. He had died without making a sound, leaving a widow and three kids.

Grim-faced, Tom set about breaking open two more of the windows that faced the street. A half-hour later, Zack Parmell arrived, carrying a ladder. He left the ladder outside and crawled through a window.

"Borrowed it from the livery," he said. "Stole it, that is. But they'll get it back. How're things in here?"

"A good spot," Shannon answered. "I wish the men in the alley had as good a fort."

"Yeah." Parmell looked through a window at the street. "But we can give 'em hell from in here. Take some of the pressure off."

Tom pushed the dust off a windowsill with his hand, then looked at Parmell. "What do you think, Zack? Will they show up?"

"We've just got no way of knowing. This might be all for nothing. But it's like my boss said, we've got to try."

"If they don't show, do you think we ought to attack their camp?"

"In my opinion, yes. It'd be like you said, some of them will get away, and we'll lose some men. I hope we don't have to do that. It'll be better if we can get them to come here."

"I've given it a lot of thought and I just don't know a better way."

"I've thought about it too. Me and V.C. talked about it most of the night, and we believe your plan is the best."

"Well"—Tom grinned a weak grin—"let's hope."

"I got to get up on the roof. If they left their camp at daylight, they could be showing up pretty soon."

"I'm guessing they left before daylight. If they left at all. They probably want to hit town, take the money, and get back to their camp before dark. It's a long day's ride from their camp to town and back."

"Yeah, you're probably right. They'd want to split the money first thing in the morning and cut for parts unknown."

Parmell crawled through the window to the plank sidewalk, picked up the ladder, and went around back to the alley. Tom heard him walking on the roof.

He waited, sneaking a look now and then through a broken window at the street. The wind whistled around the corner of the building. He cursed silently when he saw Orville and the other two sawmill hands walking down the street, carrying rifles. "Damn," he muttered, "wish to hell they'd keep those guns out of sight."

C.H. Tibalt was opening his store, using a long key to unlock a padlock as big as a man's hand. Tibalt looked nervously up and down the street before he went inside. A man in a derby hat and a plaid mackinaw opened the assay office, and an overweight woman in a plain cotton dress, black coat, and black stockings opened the laundry.

A man in jackboots clomp-clomped on the plankwalk past Tom's eye. He didn't look Tom's way.

The sun was climbing.

He smoked, stepped on his cigarette butt, rolled another. "Come on," he muttered. "Come on. Let's get this over with."

A four-up team pulling a long lumber wagon went down the street toward the sawmill, trace chains and singletrees rattling. There were no women on the street. Mary had done her job.

His hands were nervous and he couldn't keep then still. He shoved them into his pockets. "Come on, dammit."

The sun was clearly visible over the tops of the buildings. It was approaching midmorning. Another wagon pulled by two horses went down the street..

They're not coming. Shannon was afraid to admit it, but the time for them to come was passing quickly. How long would the townsmen wait? Were they nervous too? If the gang didn't show up soon, men would leave their positions and the whole plan would fail.

Shannon's chest felt hollow. His legs were weak. His backbone was turning to mush. They weren't coming. It wasn't going to work. He sat on the dusty floor and leaned back against a wall, suddenly very weary. What should he do now? Everything depended on trapping the killer gang and getting a confession out of them. Without a confession, he wouldn't be able to prove his innocence. V.C. Wheeler had said that if the plan didn't work, no one would be to blame, but Tom knew he would be blamed. Some of them would blame him. It was all over for him in Fortune.

Then he heard a sound that made him jump up. His backbone stiffened. His pulse quickened and his head began pounding. Footsteps on the roof. Hurrying footsteps.

In less than a minute, Parmell's face was at the window. "They're coming. Seven of them. Armed to the teeth."

"Spread the word, Zack. Make sure everyone is in place. Leave your rifle here." Tom's heart was beating too fast. It was going to

175

happen. Oh, Lord, he pleaded, let it go right. He saw Parmell walking rapidly down the street, saw him stop at the mercantile, go inside, come right out again and go across the street to the jail, come out and go into the vacant lot.

When he returned, Parmell crawled through the window, checked his rifle, and said, "Won't be more'n a few minutes now. I saw them come into town from the east, riding down the street. They've got those black rags around their throats, but not over their faces. They don't care who sees them."

"They're a bold bunch of sonsabitches," Shannon muttered.

"Here they come."

They rode by. Seven of them. Each man with a rifle in his hand and a six-gun on his hip.

"Bold is right," Parmell said, talking low. "They think they can just ride right into town and help themselves to anything they want."

Tom recognized Sam'l in his pillbox cap. He recognized the man named Job. He pushed his rifle barrel through the window. His finger was on the trigger, his breathing shallow. Waiting.

The seven dismounted in front of the jail, moving casually, easily. They pulled the bandannas up over their noses. Two men gathered the reins and held the horses. Five men paused at the door to the deputy's office.

"Here's where the ball begins," Tom muttered.

CHAPTER 31

One of the five put his hand on the doorknob and looked at his partners. Another nodded at him. The door was yanked open and the five poured inside.

Gunfire exploded inside the jail.

"Damn," Tom muttered. That gang knows how to do it. Rush inside immediately. Get in fast and take over. How many men did he have in there? Three. Could they drive them back out?

Parmell had his rifle to his shoulder. He squinted down the barrel and squeezed the trigger. The explosion inside the empty room hammered Tom's eardrums.

"Shit," Parmell said; "Son of a bitch moved."

Torn was taking aim. One of the men holding the horses had a six-gun in his hand, looking for someone to shoot at. Tom squeezed the trigger. This time he didn't even hear the explosion. The recoil against his cheek and shoulder was an old familiar feeling.

The man dropped face down, and the three horses he was holding stampeded down the street.

Gunfire was coming from the jail so fast and furious it all sounded like one big continuous explosion. Two men backed out, firing pistols. One dropped as shots came from across the street, from Tibalt's store. The other man spun around and snapped a shot at the store. Another ran out of the jail, grabbed for one of the remaining horses, got into the saddle, and then pitched forward onto the animal's neck. The horse reared and ran after the first three. Its rider fell off and lay still.

"Give up, you stupid sonsabitches," Tom muttered.

Instead of dropping their guns and giving up, they were shooting, glancing around for a target, shooting in all directions. They discovered that some of the gunfire was coming from Tibalt's store, and two of them turned their guns in that direction, firing as fast as they could fan the hammers of their six-guns.

Shooting from the store stopped as the men inside ducked to safety.

Now three of them were running for the vacant lot. Another grabbed for the reins of a horse, but the horses were terrified at all the noise and were rearing, plunging, pulling back The man's curses could be heard between volleys of gunfire as he tried to mount. Then the horse went down, first onto its knees and then onto its side, a bullet through the heart. The man ran for the vacant lot and joined the remaining three of his partners.

"Get 'em," Tom yelled, firing as rapidly as he could aim, squeeze the trigger, and jack the lever down on his rifle. When the hammer clicked harmlessly, he yanked a handful of cartridges from his jacket pocket and reloaded, willing his fingers to move faster.

One of the four fell. Tom didn't know who shot him. The other three managed to get into the lot out of sight of the bank windows.

"They need help," Tom yelled. "Stay here, Zack. Don't let 'em get by you." He crawled through the window, hanging onto his rifle.

Tom ran behind the bank to the alley, started running down the alley. He saw Orville standing behind the jail, firing around the corner. Orville stepped away from the building to take better aim, then suddenly threw his gun up, spun around and fell.

"Damn," Tom said through his teeth. "Dammit all anyway." He ran, afraid now that three of them would get through the vacant lot, hoping to get a shot at them first.

A mixture of rifle and pistol fire popped, boomed, crashed. It was the battle at Shiloh all over again. The scene flashed through Tom's mind as he ran. Hardee's attack faltered, losing the fight. Then Bragg's Corps swept into the battle like a tornado, screaming the rebel yell. The Feds' stand collapsed.

One of Orville's partners stumbled and fell. His hat went

spinning. He dropped his rifle and grabbed his head with both hands. That left only one man guarding the vacant lot.

Tom got there in time to hear Sam'l let out a wild rebel yell and charge recklessly through the lot, not shooting, just running. Tom jerked to a stop, threw his rifle to his shoulder, and fired. He thought he'd missed and he jacked another cartridge into the firing chamber. Sam'l fell onto his knees, rolled over, got up, and snapped a shot at Tom. His shot was hasty, and the lead whistled past Tom's left ear. Tom still had his rifle to his shoulder.

Sam'l screamed, "Don't shoot. Don't shoot. For God's sake, don't shoot." He was on his knees trying to stand. He sat down hard.

Tom had him in his sights, his finger on the trigger. "Drop your gun. Throw it away."

Sam'l threw his six-gun down in the weeds and sat on the ground, holding his left leg in his hands. Tom ran past him into the vacant lot. The shooting had stopped. Two men, including Tibalt, came out of the store across the street, carrying rifles.

"Where are they?" Tom yelled. "Did we get 'em all?"

"I don't think so," a man yelled back.

"No. Two of 'em are runnin' east. Get after 'em."

Gunshots came from the end of the block, and Tom ran into the street and saw them. There were two of them trying to go down the street. Tom pleaded silently, not so fast, Zack. Take aim. Take aim, Zack.

One of the two dropped to one knee, sighted along a rifle barrel, and fired. Then he jumped up and ran. Shannon ran after him. A volley of shots came from behind Tom, and the other man fell, rolled over on his back, and lay still.

Now it was a footrace. The outlaw looked back over his shoulder, saw Tom behind him, spun, and fired his rifle from the hip. The bullet hit the dirt in front of Tom's feet. He stopped and raised his rifle, but before he could fire the man disappeared around a corner of the bank building.

And then Tom realized that no more shots were coming from the bank.

"Damn," he muttered. "Dammit." He ran to the corner, saw the outlaw pointing his rifle at a townsman on a horse, saw the townsman

179

raise one hand and step off the horse. Tom ran around the corner, trying to get a clear shot before the outlaw could get on horseback. He stopped, took aim. The horse was jumping and the outlaw was trying to get his foot in the stirrup and hang onto his rifle at the same time. He dropped the rifle and got mounted. Tom fired.

But the plunging horse spoiled his aim. He quickly shoved the lever down to reload, and for a few seconds the lever stuck. The spent shell casing was still in the gun. "Dammit," Tom swore.

The horse was running now with the outlaw on its back, heading north out of town. Cursing, Tom jerked the reloading mechanism, and finally used his fingers to flip the spent casing out. Then he levered in another round.

The outlaw was spurring hard, riding recklessly. The gun at his shoulder again, Tom took aim. Careful aim. Got the man's broad back in the sights. One shot was all he would get.

Squeezed the trigger.

Again he thought he had missed, and he cursed. Then the horse ducked sharply to the left and the man was pitched off the right side. He hit the ground hard enough to bounce once.

Two townsmen ran up beside Shannon. "Did you get 'im?"

"I think so. He's not moving."

"He's hit, all right."

"I'll go take a look."

"Watch him," Tom warned. "He could be playing dead."

"I'll watch 'im."

Tom turned. A crowd had gathered. Everyone was yelling, excited, guns in their hands, looking for something to shoot at. Tom went back to the street in front of the bank building. The crowd followed. Men were running up from all directions, yelling, "What happened? Who's doin all the shootin'? What in hell's going on? Is that Tom Shannon? What in hell's he doin here? It's him, all right. Don't shoot. He's on our side."

Tom looked through the crowd for a familiar face. He saw C.H. Tibalt and Hugh March. Then he saw V.C. Wheeler and his cowhand named Shorty.

"Where's Zack?" Tom asked.

"Don't know." Wheeler was out of breath from running.

Excitement held his voice at a high octave. "Haven't seen him."

Yanking boards loose from windows, Tom peered inside the bank. He let out a groan when he saw Parmell lying on his side on the dusty floor. Quickly, he scrambled through the window.

Shorty was right behind him.

He knew when he got close that Parmell was dead. A bullet had taken off the side of his head.

"Oh no," Torn groaned. "My God, no." He dropped to his knees beside the body. He felt like crying.

Two more men climbed through the window. They stood over the body several long moments, then one said, "Let's git 'im outside." More boards were torn off the window, and the remainder of the glass was broken out. They passed Parmell's body outside where it was laid gently on the plankwalk. Tom took off his jacket and covered Parmell's face and the misshapen head.

CHAPTER 32

Down the block, men were still shouting, excited. "Who done it?" someone yelled. "Who done all the shootin'?" It looked to Tom as though all the men in Fortune were gathered on the street now. They were milling like a bunch of excited sheep, going nowhere, hollering at each other. Then Tibalt yelled, "Let's gather 'em up, boys," and they started picking up bodies and laying them on the walk in front of the jail.

Two men carried up the body of the man Tom had shot off the horse. They were breathing hard from the exertion. "Got 'im plumb center," one of them said. "This's the last of 'em."

"Are they all dead?"

"Six of 'em dead and one shot in the leg."

"Where's Orville?" Tom asked.

"He got hit. In the right side. Slug plowed into 'im but missed the important parts. He'll be all right if we can get 'im to a doctor."

"Stage's due in an hour. They got relay stops and can change horses. Put 'im on the stage, and he'll get to the doctor at Fairplay tonight."

"That's the fastest way, all right."

Orville was sitting in the weeds, propped against the side of the jail building. He grinned through his beard when he saw Tom approaching. "Got 'em all, didn't we, Shannon. Got ever' damned one of 'em."

"We sure did, Orville. We're going to get you to a doctor at

182

Fairplay,"

"It was worth it, Shannon. No matter what happens to me it was damn well worth it." Orville tipped his head back and let out a yell. "Whooee, we got them sombitches. We got ever' damned one of 'em."

"Stay still, Orville. Save your strength."

Women were hurrying up now, holding onto their long skirts. Among them was Mary. She stopped, glanced through the crowd. "Where's Tom?" Her voice was high, excited, fearful. "Where's Tom Shannon?" She saw him then and ran to him. "Tom. Are you hurt?" Her arms went around him and she buried her face in his chest.

"No. I'm one of the lucky ones, Mary."

"Oh, thank God."

He pulled back, looked into her face. "We lost Zack Parmell."

"Oh, Tom, I'm so sorry."

"Orville's been hit too."

She spotted Orville then and hurried to him. "Oh Orville, where...?"

"Ain't nothin', Mary. Just went in right here"—he pointed to a spot of blood on his shirt—"without hittin' nothin' but fat. I'll live to see you and Tom Shannon married."

"You need a doctor, Orville."

"We're puttin' 'im in the stage and sendin' 'im to Fairplay," someone said. "He's gonna be all right."

Orville grinned through his beard. "I'm too damned mean to die."

Tom turned to the crowd and asked, "Anyone else hurt?"

"Look at this."

Tom turned to see who was talking. It was one of Orville's partners. He was holding his hat in one hand and had a finger of the other hand poked through a hole in the crown. "A inch closer and I'd be layin' over there too."

"Man, that was close," someone said.

"I heared it and I felt it and I done thought I was dead for sure. Scared the peewadin' out of me."

"Are you sure you weren't hit?" Tom asked.

"Nossir." He ran his hand over the top of his head. "Not a

scratch."

"Those men in the alley here did a very commendable job, Shannon." It was V.C. Wheeler speaking.

"That they did. They had so much lead coming at them...most men would have just ducked and covered up their heads. They stood their ground and kept four of the gang from getting away. Uh, Mr. Wheeler, I'm terribly sorry about Zack. He was a good man. He and I could have been good friends."

Wheeler looked down at the weeds under his boots and spoke with reverence, "He was a good soldier. He did his duty."

Mary was kneeling beside Orville. "Can't we take him someplace where, he'll be more comfortable?"

"Best not move him, Mrs. Cress."

She took off her wool sweater and put it behind Orville's head. "I'll run and get you a blanket."

"Don't bother, Mary. I'm just fine and dandy."

The crowd was milling again, still asking what happened. Someone said, "How many're dead?"

"Six. Another'n got a ball in the leg."

"Seven, countin' Zack Parmell."

"Got all of that gang of killers, howsomever."

"Which one is still alive?"

"That 'un over there."

Tom looked where the man was pointing. Sam'l was sitting on the plankwalk beside the bodies of his partners. His head was down between his knees and he was holding his left calf in both hands. Blood was oozing between his fingers.

"Sam'l?"

The man looked up at Tom. His lips skinned back in a weak smile. "You laid a trap fer us far and squar', Cap'n."

The crowd gathered around.

"How many of you were there, Sam'l?"

"I had a chance to put a slug in you once, Cap'n. Shoulda done it."

"How many of you were there?"

"Ain't no use askin' me no questions. It's agin my principles to blow agin my pards."

"That means there are more," someone said.

"How many more, Sam'l?"

"You got us, Cap'n."

"No," Tom said, "I think there's another. Is that right, Sam'l?"

The man's Adam's apple bobbed and he tried another weak grin. "You're dead center, Cap'n."

"Who is he?"

"I ain't blowin' agin my pards."

"Let's hang 'im," someone yelled. "Who's got a rope?"

"We got the gallows all ready for 'im."

"No." Tom looked around at the crowd. "He's entitled to a trial."

The crowd quieted. Only a few angry murmurs were spoken. Tom squatted in front of Sam'l.

"Tell me one thing. Who killed Scott Wheeler?"

Sam'l nodded his head in the direction of the bodies. "That 'un over there. Only name I knowed 'im by was Job."

"Are you sure about that?" V.C. Wheeler was squatting beside Tom. "You, can't be mistaken?"

"Nope. The cap'n here didn't do it. It was Job."

"Why?"

"He was tole to."

"Who told him to?"

The weak grin returned. "I ain't blowin' agin my pards."

"But you just pointed out that man there as the one who killed my son."

"He don't care. He's dead."

"Are you saying..." Tom spoke slowly, carefully. "Are you saying the man who told Job to kill Scott Wheeler is still alive?"

"I ain't blowin' agin my pards."

"Why was my son killed?"

"He knowed too much."

"Knew too much. What did he know?"

Sam'l shook his head. "Are you gonna fetch a doctor? My laig's shot to hell."

C.H. Tibalt took a biscuit-sized watch out of a vest pocket and snapped open the lid. "Stage'll be here pretty soon. Are we going to send him to the doctor too?"

"No, by God." It was the sawmill worker with a hole in his hat. "We're sendin Orville on the stage, and this son of a bitch ain't fit to ride in the same wagon with him."

Tom stood and took Wheeler by the arm. "I think I know the answer to your question. I think I know who the last one of them is."

"Who?"

Tom looked around, trying to find the face that was etched in his mind.

"Speak up, man."

Tibalt had overheard the conversation, and he too stood in front of Tom. "Do you know more than you've told us, Shannon?"

"I've got a strong suspicion."

"Spill it, Shannon."

Tom spotted the man. He was hanging back in the crowd, listening but not speaking. He was a tall, lean man with a silver-belly hat, a thin moustache, flowery vest, and pearl-handled pistol low on his hip. Tom handed his rifle to Wheeler and shifted his gunbelt to a familiar position. He put his right hand on the six-gun butt, summoned his courage. The tall, thin man was a professional gunslinger, a cold, calculating killer. He carried his gun low for a fast draw. He saw Tom eyeing him, glanced around as if looking for a way to escape, saw there was no escape, and stood still, waiting. Tom started walking through the crowd toward him. Wheeler and Tibalt followed. Mary interrupted.

"Tom, I'm going to get a blanket and a pillow for Orville. I can't just leave him there in the weeds. I—" She stopped talking abruptly when she saw the determined set of his jaw, saw where he was looking. Horror spread over her face as she realized what was happening. "Tom, I...Tom, don't."

CHAPTER 33

Tom Shannon glanced at Mary and spoke softly, "I've got to."

"Tom, please. He'll kill you."

He walked with slow, deliberate steps. The man stood his ground, spraddle-legged, ready.

"Tom." Mary hurried through the crowd ahead of him. She stopped beside the man.

"Move away, Mary."

"Tom, please."

Then he was no more than fifteen feet in front of the mart. Their eyes locked.

"Him?" Wheeler asked.

"Yeah, him." Tom's eyes held the man's eyes.

"Why him?"

For a few seconds, Tom didn't answer. Then he spoke carefully. "You're Henry Barrett. You deal faro and any other card game you can get anyone into. You hear everything in the Salty Dog saloon. You've got spies in the bank at Fairplay and at Tarryall. There's not much you don't hear."

Everyone was quiet now, listening. Barrett's eyes didn't change. He didn't move.

Tom continued. "You were playing cards with Scott Wheeler that night. Just you and Scott Wheeler. You were worried about him. He'd seen you up there in the high country, heading back from the outlaw camp. You told him you were elk hunting, and that was a lie.

187

You've got no use for elk meat. You take your meals at the Silver Lode."

Still, Barrett didn't move. His right hand hovered over the gun on his hip.

"On your way back from the gang's camp, you stopped at my cabin, went in, and picked up one of my used percussion caps. You thought it might come in handy sometime."

Finally, Barrett spoke. "You don't believe any of this, do you?" His eyes went over the crowd and stopped at V.C. Wheeler. "Tom Shannon shot your kid in the back and he's trying to put the blame on me."

Tom's eyes didn't waver. "You were afraid Scott Wheeler would get suspicious sooner or later, and you decided he had to die. You got your chance a couple of nights later. You and young Wheeler were playing cards, just the two of you. Job over there came in to tell you about the stage carrying gold. He whispered, but Wheeler overheard part of it. Wheeler knew he'd heard something he wasn't supposed to hear, and he quit playing cards and went to the bar. That's when you told Job to go outside and wait for him. Shoot him. Wheeler had a drink at the bar, decided to tell Deputy Atwell what he suspected, and left. When the shots were heard and men gathered around the body, you dropped one of my caps on the ground where it would be found."

A murmur went through the crowd at Tom's back. Wheeler said, "What do you say to that, Barrett?"

Barrett's thin lips barely moved. "He's a liar."

"No." Tom's heart was pounding again. He was no fast-draw gunman. He could die right here, right now. He spoke through his teeth. "You're the liar, Barrett."

Men stepped aside. Gunfire was about to erupt again. Somebody was going to die. Men stepped back out of the way. But not Mary.

"Please," she said to the crowd, "won't you help him. He helped all of you. Don't let him be killed now."

No one moved. Tibalt spoke, but his voice was uncertain. "See here, now. We've had enough killing. We..." He didn't finish.

Out of the corner of his eyes, Tom saw Mary shift toward

Barrett and stand beside him.

"Get away, Mary." He didn't dare look at her. Barrett's lips barely moved and his voice was full of death as he said, "Nobody calls me a liar and lives to tell about it."

"Get away, Mary."

The gambler's hand was a blur. The pearl-handled pistol was in it. Shannon grabbed for his own gun. He was too late. The gambler's gun was coming up, and Tom saw death.

But the first shot hit the ground.

Mary had shoved him. Just put her hands against his right shoulder and shoved as hard as she could. Barrett staggered sideways to keep his balance. Then he hit her in the face with his left fist. She fell back.

Tom's gun was clear and level. He held the trigger and fanned the hammer with the edge of his left hand. The big pistol boomed and bucked. The gambler's left leg was knocked from under him and he jerked forward onto his knees. A grimace spread his lips as his gun came up a second time. It was one of the new single-action revolvers, the kind that didn't have to be cocked. Tom fanned the hammer of his gun again. Barrett dropped flat on his face. His fine silver-belly hat went rolling until it stopped at someone's feet.

No one noticed, but dark clouds had drifted over from the west and had blocked out the sun. Everyone was quiet. Tom holstered his gun and went to Mary, who was standing unsteadily, holding one hand to her face. With his fingertips he touched her rapidly-swelling left eye.

"We'd better get you home and do something about that."

"Yes, Tom. Can we go home now?"

The crowd stepped back as they made their way through, arms around each other. At her house he found some salve and spread it with gentle fingers over her eye. The eye was turning purple.

His hands were steady and he knew they shouldn't be. He had just killed at least three men and wounded another. But instead of feeling nervous, excited, he was depressed. It was the old post-battle depression he had felt before. Now was the time for taking care of the wounded and writing letters to the kin of the dead. As an officer, he had done his share of the letter writing.

Mary was trembling, tears running down her face. She was no hardened war veteran. He held her tight and tried to stop her trembling.

Her voice was muffled against his chest. "As...as long as I live, Tom, I will never forget what I saw this morning."

"No, Mary," he sighed. "You won't forget it, but you'll learn to live with the memory."

"The bodies. Their faces looked like the faces of normal men, the kind of men who come into the Silver Lode. In death, they looked like ordinary men."

He hugged her tight.

"I wonder if any of them had families."

"Probably not. They were outlaws. Killers and thieves. Even rapists."

She looked into his face. "You were in the war, Tom. How did you erase it from your mind?"

"You can't. Not ever. This is...I've seen the dead and wounded strewn over the battlefields. Haversacks and canteens and rifles scattered among the bodies. Legs and arms blown off. I've heard the cries of the wounded, begging to be shot and put out of their misery. I've seen..." He swallowed a lump that had formed in his throat.

"Tom," she said sharply. "Tom."

He stopped talking and brought his mind back to the present.

"I'm sorry, Tom. I'm behaving like a child."

"No, you're not. I can tell you...anyone who thinks there is glory in battle is either inhuman or has never been on a battlefield. You're not behaving like a child, Mary. I've seen grown men break down and cry like a baby. I've even—"

"Tom." She was running her fingertips over his face. "Poor darling."

He realized then that his whole body was tense. Every nerve and muscle was tight. Now his hands were shaking.

"My poor Tom."

Ordering himself to relax, he let his breath out slowly, stepped back, and sighed. "You won't ever forget what happened today, Mary, but you will learn to live with it. You'll learn not to let it bother you."

"Yes, we have to go on with our lives."

After a moment of silence, he said, "I've got to go back. I started this mess and I've got to help clean it up. I'll be back as soon as I can."

"I have to go too. The Silver Lode will be busy and I'll be needed."

Forcing a grin, he said, "I hope you can work with one eye, because you won't be seeing out of this one for a while."

She grinned too. "I've done that work so much I can do it with both eyes shut."

Back on the street, Shannon saw the crowd still there. Now they were not milling. Instead they were all facing the vacant lot next to the jail. The gallows.

Sam'l was standing on the trapdoor, a hangman's noose around his neck. The knot with thirteen wraps was on the left side of his neck where it would hammer him behind the ear. He was standing on one foot while two men, one on each side of the trapdoor, held him up by the shoulders. His hands were bound behind his back.

Tom shouted, "No, wait." No one paid any attention to him. He tried to push his way through. "Stop. Wait."

Sam'l threw his head back and let out a wild, rebel "Heee-yooo." His voice displayed no fear as he yelled, "Save your Jeff Davis dollars, boys, the South's gonna rise again. God bless ever'body and let 'er rip."

"Stop," Tom pleaded.

The trapdoor sprung open. Sam'l plummeted through and hit the end of the rope. His neck broke with a loud snap. The body hung limp.

Shannon stood alone while the crowd gathered around the gallows, took the body down, carried it to the plankwalk in front of the jail, and laid it out with the seven others.

Someone said, "We've got a lot of buryin' to do."

"Best get it done before dark. The ground's gonna freeze tonight for sure."

"Let's get a wagon and some shovels. We'll all work on it."

Some of the men walked away, going after digging tools and a wagon. C.H. Tibalt came up to Tom, faced him. "This town will be peaceful now. It's a good place to live and do business again. The good people will come back."

"That's right." Hugh March came up too. "But we need a deputy marshal. How about you, Tom? It won't be such a bad job now. And you know that if you need help, we'll all help. You can count on us."

"Yeah." Tom swallowed hard. "You're dependable men, but...I don't know. I can't think of myself as a lawman. Besides, only the marshal can appoint a deputy."

"He'll be here tomorrow when he hears about what happened. He'll appoint anybody we tell him to appoint."

"The job's yours if you want it, Tom."

"I don't know. I appreciate the offer, but..."

V.C. Wheeler joined them. "I've got another offer. I need a foreman. You've run cattle in this territory long enough to know what to do, Tom, and you're a leader. You've proven that. I've got a good house at the ranch that you and Mary can live in, and you can run your cattle on the same grass and draw good wages at the same time."

"Well, thanks, but—"

"There'll come a time when we have to divide up the grazing land around here, but we're both honest, reasonable men and we can work it out."

"I sure do appreciate the offer, Mr. Wheeler. I'd like to think about it."

"Sure. Think about it. The job's yours anytime you want it."

At Mary's house again, he prowled through the rooms, wishing Mary were there. He carried water to his horse, noted that enough grazing was left in Mary's back yard to last a couple more days, and went back inside the house.

When Mary came home, he kissed her swollen eye and made her sit down while he fixed his own supper. She had eaten at the cafe and wasn't hungry. While he ate he told her about the job offers.

"You've got several options, Tom. You can be a deputy marshal, and I've heard the pay is good, or you can be a ranch foreman, or you can go back to doing what you were doing. You can graze your cattle close to town here and work in the timber for extra money, and you can live in a comfortable house in town. The house I bought in your name has a stable where you can keep your horses. In the spring, you can build a brand new house on your homestead. You can—"

He interrupted, "Yeah, I can do all that, and we'll have to talk about it and make some plans. And I'll have to lead some men to the outlaws' camp. No telling what we'll find there. But there's another thing I'm going to do for sure, and as soon as possible."

"What's that?"

"I'm going to take you to Fairplay and hunt up a preacher and we're going to get married."

Her swollen eye was purple and blue now, and her smile was a little lopsided. "You didn't know it, Mr. Shannon, but those words just prevented the biggest battle of your life."

Outside the house, a cold wind whipped down off the mountains and a light snow flew almost horizontally. Gradually, the snow picked up in volume and the first real storm of the season was under way.

Inside, they blew out the lamps and went to bed.

THE END

Be sure to check out the next novel in
Doyle Trent's Tales of the Old Wild West series:

RUSTLER'S TRAIL

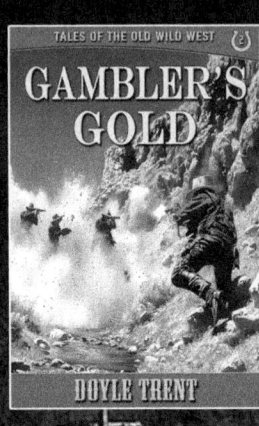
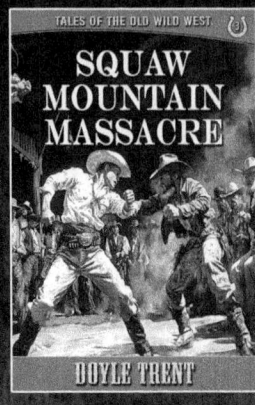

LOOKING FOR ACTION & ADVENTURE
AUTHOR ALAN CAILLOU
DELIVERS !

ADDITIONAL ACTION & ADVENTURE
FROM ALAN CAILLOU

DON'T MISS ANY OF NEIL HUNTER'S NOVELS FROM CALIBER BOOKS

Reporter Les Mason is completing an expose on the Long Point Nuclear Plant. But before he can finish he dies an agonizing death. The doctors are baffled—and there are similar cases to follow...Chris Lane, his girlfriend, and organizer of the Long Point Protestors, discovers Mason's notes, and decides to find out for herself what the plant has to hide.

2 BOOK SERIES

In middle of the 21st century America – over-populated decaying cities are ruled by hi-tech gangs pushing every vice and wastelands are controlled by bands of mutants. Ordinary citizens are oppressed and face a hopeless future. But Marshal T.J. Cade is a new breed of law enforcer. Teamed with his cyborg partner, Janek, Cade takes on these criminals and works in the gray areas of the law to get the job done.

3 BOOK SERIES

The village of Shepthorne England wasn't being gripped, but strangled by a winter's blanket of heavy snow and Arctic temperatures. The trouble began innocently enough with a massive pile-up of autos on frozen roads leading to and from the village. Then, from the sky, a military transport plane with its top secret cargo of devastation crashed down towards the center of the village. Hell was just beginning to touch Shepthorne and its unsuspecting citizens...

FROM CALIBER BOOKS

CALIBER BOOKS

www.calibercomics.com

FROM FANTASY AND SCIENCE FICTION
AUTHOR ROLAND J. GREEN
THREE EPIC SERIES

FROM CALIBER BOOKS IN PAPERBACK AND EBOOK